Rialta

RETRIBUTION KINGS #2

ELLA MILES

Retribution Kings Series

Lennox (Book 1)
Rialta (Book 2)

Hayes (Book 3)
Lilith (Book 4)

Gage (Book 5)
Nova (Book 6)

The Retribution Kings Series is a spinoff of the Retribution Games Series. If you want to read Beckett and River's story, start with Mistaken Hero

CHAPTER 1

Lennox

MY SHOULDERS ARE SCREAMING in agony—stretched to their limits above my head, holding the weight of my body as my toes barely touch the ground. There's an intense pounding in my head, and I feel like I could sleep for a month straight.

But I'm alive.

Most people's reaction in this situation would be to jolt awake and start thinking of an escape plan. But I know better than to alert anyone watching me that I'm awake until I have a plan. So I stay calm, keeping my heartbeat and breath steady.

My shirt is gone, but at least they left my pants on this time. The scratchy fabric digging into my wrists tells me they used rope to bind me. The question, is who are *they*?

I try to remember what happened the last time I was conscious, but my memories are foggy. Any one of my numerous enemies could have done this—Vincent, any of the Corsi men, the Retribution Kings, or the still unknown man who wants Rialta dead.

Rialta—I remember Rialta. Suddenly her memory knocks the breath out of me.

I hurt her.

I killed Kit.

At least, I think I did. That's what she accused me of, and it seems like something I'd do. My memories aren't giving me any clues at the moment—they're completely consumed by Rialta. The pain etched on her face, the tears freely flowing, the way Andrea kissed her cheek, and she didn't flinch away.

Rialta drugged me—that's how much she hates me.

I love her.

Fucking dammit, I love her.

Falling in love was the one thing that could have saved us, and it was too late. And yet, me loving her will also destroy her.

I won't live—not long enough to give her a happily ever after. If I somehow got her to love me, too, my death would destroy her. I should know—loving someone in my past destroyed me.

Who am I kidding? Rialta could never love me, especially after what I did to Kit. I'm her enemy, the villain in her story. And yet somehow, against all odds, I fell in love with her.

So why would I sabotage that by killing Kit?

To ensure she could never love me?

To protect her since Vincent is bound to kill me for failing to live up to his challenge?

I don't know.

I don't remember.

I need to find a way to escape. But not until I see Rialta, not until I know the truth. It can't be true. She can't be with Andrea. She can't hate me that much.

Except she always hated me, at least until I thought she loved me.

"We know you're awake," I hear Andrea say as footsteps near.

I raise my head, no longer pretending, and stare straight into his bloodthirsty eyes. A dozen men surround him in the dark basement they've tied me up in. But none of them is what strikes fear through my soul.

Rialta Corsi—my wife. The woman whose last name I took. The woman who I vowed to protect, to fall in love with, and to end her attacker's life. The woman who I hated but somehow fell madly in love with is standing next to him, leaning on him for support.

My eyes lock in on hers, looking for any sign she's on my side. This is all a mistake. She's been coerced. She still likes me, wants me, maybe—somehow, she fell in love with me the same way I fell in love with her.

All I see is hate.

It's a hatred I've never felt from her before, even when Vincent and I forced her to marry me. Even when we were playing our silly games together, she's never hated me like this.

And I've never loved like this—even before her, it's never felt like this. I've never loved this deeply, and that scares the fuck out of me. I know how hard it was to recover from losing someone I loved before. If I lost Rialta—fuck, I can't think about it. It would be like falling into the deepest parts of hell. And the person I'd become would wipe out the rest of humanity on Earth.

If she hates me, that's fine. I don't need her to love me. I just need her to still be mine.

I want to rip Andrea's arm from her shoulders. I want to throw her over my shoulder caveman-style and tell her she's mine. Tell her I love her and that I'd do anything for her. I'd even let her be with someone I hate, someone like Andrea, if that's what she really wants. I just need her to know in my heart she'll forever be mine—the woman I love. The woman I'd die for. No matter how much she hates me.

Is this really how she feels? I need to know the truth. I need to know if she's always been scheming against me. If Andrea and her have been friends or even lovers before. She loved Kit, but was he the only man she loved?

I pour my heart into my expression as I look at her. I'm not angry with her for what she did. If I did kill Kit, I deserve this. Even if he was wrong for her, I should have never hurt her in this way. It's unforgivable, and I want her to know that.

But Andrea is a power-hungry man. He'll do whatever it takes to take over her father's empire. He'll do worse than just force her into a marriage—he'll rape her, torture her, and worse to get what he wants from her.

I know evil, being evil myself. And Andrea is evil. Whereas I have my limits with people I love, Andrea doesn't. He only loves power.

Rialta doesn't change her reaction. She doesn't look at me as if I'm anything but scum.

Andrea turns and whispers something in her ear.

She nods solemnly and takes a step back into the shadows of the basement and out of my sight. It's one of the greatest ways he could torture me. I can't communicate with her. The only thing worse would be torturing her himself.

The only thing I can be comforted by is that Andrea won't hurt her yet. He needs Vincent to agree to let him marry her after he kills me. And Vincent won't let him do that if he hurts her. And if he doesn't marry Rialta, then he doesn't get Vincent's power.

That means there's nothing Andrea can do to hurt me.

He walks toward me as his men stand around the room smirking, anticipating enjoying what he's going to do to me.

"It took you long enough to wake up. I was afraid my dear Rialta might have overdosed you."

I smirk. "Vincent hasn't given you permission to kill me yet. He'd kill you for not following his orders."

Andrea's nostrils flare—I struck a nerve. "No. After he sees all the evidence I have against you, Vincent would be happy for me to kill you. But then I couldn't torture you and get revenge for Rialta. You killed the love of her life. You should pay with more than your life."

Andrea doesn't give a damn that I killed Kit or hurt Rialta, but there is no use arguing with him. The men in this room are Corsi men, and I can't appear weak in front of them. Andrea is a backstabbing, ruthless bastard who only cares about himself. I'm sure he's already betrayed some in this room. I need them to see I'm worthy of saving. I'm on their side, and I would help them. If I look weak, no one will think I'm worthy of being the next Corsi leader.

When I don't respond, Andrea grows impatient. He walks over to the wall behind me. I don't have to look to know there are all kinds of devices meant to torture me with.

I don't know what Andrea's past is, what has made him who he is today, and why Vincent wouldn't choose him for Rialta in the first place. But none of that matters.

"This is for Rialta," Andrea says menacingly a second before a whip strikes my back.

My body jerks forward, and my skin burns immediately as the familiar touch of leather hits my skin but doesn't break it open yet. Andrea put all his fury into that strike, but the anger made him lose control. It takes some finesse and practice to use a whip to inflict the most amount of pain. Although I'm sure he'll strike me long enough to find his stride.

It's effortless for me to keep quiet as he strikes me again and again. The first dozen blows are weak and won't even leave a lasting mark.

Instead, I stare into the black void in the direction of where I hope Rialta is standing and watching.

I don't know how she's feeling. *Is she enjoying watching Andrea get revenge for her? Does she feel this is justice, or...?*

I stop myself from hoping this is all a farce. She can't really care about me, especially if I really did kill Kit. If I did kill him, I'm sure I had a good reason. She was mine. I could feel it. I could feel her falling for me, wanting me. Kit didn't matter. He was gone. She had let him go and forgotten about him.

Killing Kit would have only hurt my cause. *So why did I do it?*

Everything's foggy. It will take time for me to remember what happened. But I will, and when I do, I'll have a chance to win her back. If my action hurt her this badly, I did it for a purpose. I had already fallen for her at that point. And as much as I hated her ex, I would have never hurt her like that without cause.

Now isn't the time to tell her that. Now is the time to listen, to figure out where her head is and what she wants from me. *Does she truly want me dead or not?*

Suddenly, Andrea finally breaks my skin. I can feel my warm blood running down my back. The burning intensifies as he strikes me again, and more blood flows. It hurts. It feels like he's tearing my back apart, ripping every piece of flesh from my body.

But it won't break me.

I've been here before—felt like I was going to die. Like I couldn't survive the pain. Knowing I'd pass out because my body couldn't register more.

If anyone looked closely, they'd see the scars hidden

beneath the tattoos. They'd see the torture I've been through. They'd know what I can endure because I have before.

And staring into the darkness, knowing I have to survive this for her, it gives me even more strength to be able to endure, suffer, survive.

My body sways with every strike, but I don't cry, yell, or scream. I don't react at all except to think of my wife and how I'll do anything for her. I deserve this. Even if I had a good reason to kill Kit, I still hurt her. And I deserve every punishment I'm about to go through.

I hear Andrea getting frustrated behind me. He wants me to cry and beg for him to stop. He wants me to show how weak I am and how strong he is.

Last time I went through something like this, I lost the woman I loved while I was breaking. This time the woman I love is hidden in the darkness, and she won't die tonight. No matter what happens, he won't kill her.

Nothing Andrea does to me now will be as bad as that night. He can't hurt me—at least not in a way that will leave any permanent damage on my heart.

"Your turn," I hear Andrea say, passing the whip to one of his men.

The crack rings around the room as the whip is snapped against my back with a different, more skilled force than Andrea. This man is going to rip my back apart until my muscles and bones are poking through my skin.

My eyes stay wide open as I stare at where I know Rialta is.

I love you.

I'm sorry.

I wish I could say those words out loud, but if I open my mouth I'll scream, and I won't give them the satisfaction. Plus, I don't want the first time I tell her I love her to be while I'm bleeding out in a room full of men. She deserves the first time to be romantic. She deserves a lot. She deserves better than me, better than this.

I want to read her mind. I wish I knew what was going through her head. *Is she satisfied with the revenge they are inflicting? Does she want them to go further? Does she want me dead?*

When there is nothing left for them to strike on my bloody and raw back, Andrea sends another man to hurt me with his fists.

With a growl, he lands his first blow on my jaw. A tooth comes loose as blood floods my mouth, and my head snaps to the side, away from Rialta. He punches me in the gut next, taking all the air from my body as I try to double over but can't.

Rialta.

Why didn't I realize it sooner? Why didn't I tell you before? Why didn't I tell you everything? Why did I think I couldn't love when the only person I could truly love was right in front of me? I could have loved you all this time. Then if I died now it would have been worth it. I would have died having loved you. I would have found a way to ensure your safety.

I'm not sorry for falling in love with you. I should be. I vowed I'd never experience that pain again, but I'm not sorry. I'm just sorry that I don't know if I can save you.

Even if I survive, there's no guarantee. Even if you forgive me, it probably won't be enough. As much as I try to protect people, I always fail. Everyone I've ever loved has died, and Rialta will be no different.

No, I'll find a way to save her.

But do I even really know her?

Another man takes his turn slicing into my skin with a knife. Then another with a cigar to my chest. Each man in the room takes their turn torturing me. Every one but her. The woman I know wouldn't stand by and watch. She'd want to get revenge herself.

"It's your turn, Rialta. Get your retribution," I sputter through the blood.

I'm not sure if she'll listen. I'm not sure if Andrea will even let her. But I know she's still in this room, and I need to see her. I need to know how she really feels.

My head has fallen down—I no longer have the strength to hold it up. Blood and sweat drip over my eyes, making it hard to see. I wheeze with every breath. There isn't a place on my body that isn't bloodied, bruised, or marked. I'll have scars that last a lifetime from this to add to the ones I already have. The tattoos I have will continue to hide most of the scars, but the wound on my heart—reopened and bigger than ever before—will never close.

There's a long pause as the room is silent after my request. All eyes are turned to Rialta to see what she's going to do.

With all of the strength left in my body, I lift my head and stare into the shadows where I know she is.

It's only then that she takes a step into the light.

I can barely see her through the blood and sweat, but I can see her pain. She's in absolute agony. She's wearing her heart on her chest. And yet, she's never looked stronger. There are no tears, no trembling, no hesitation. I can see the determination on her face. She knows exactly what she's going to do next.

She walks toward me—each step deliberate and strong.

I hold her gaze, refusing to drop my head or even blink. I don't know how much time I have left on this earth, but I'm not going to spend a second of it not loving her. Even if I can't tell her yet, and even if she's going to hate me for the rest of her life.

She stops just in front of me—staring at me with an intensity I've never seen on her face before. But I can't read her mind. I don't know what she's trying to tell me, or if she's even trying to tell me anything. I'm just delusional. All she wants to tell me is how much she hates me.

She looks past me and holds out her hand. I can't turn my head to see what she's asking for.

"Why did you kill Kit?" she asks.

She waits, but I don't say anything.

She shakes her head. "You're really not going to tell me? Don't you think you owe me an explanation?"

I don't say anything. There is nothing I could say right now to help her, and if she needs to be angry, to get revenge in order to survive her pain, then that's the only way I can help her. I don't know why I killed Kit. And even if I did, the explanation won't help her—the anger will. She needs to be furious until she can handle her grief.

I see what's in her hand a second before she thrusts the metal tip into my chest.

"I'll leave this here until you remember," she hisses into my ear.

She turns and walks away, leaving the knife in my chest. Even though she's literally going to be the death of me, I think I love her even more.

Rialta

MY HAND TREMBLES as I walk away from Lennox, but I don't look back. And I do everything I can to stop thinking as I walk up the basement stairs. When I reach the top, light floods me as I open the door and step into the main kitchen of Andrea's mansion.

I'm shaking with every step, and I'm about to pass out. All I want to do is flee upstairs to the bedroom Andrea assigned me and sleep. Unconsciousness is the only way to escape my grief.

I try not to think about *him*, but it's impossible. He was the love of my life. He was my everything. And...

"You okay, Rialta?" Andrea asks from behind me. Several of his men come into the kitchen from the stairs and watch us closely. I find that Andrea always has an audience, and therefore so do I.

I silently nod, not trusting my words at this moment.

He studies me closely. "You were incredibly strong down there. Most women wouldn't want to watch, let alone participate in the gory parts of the job."

I glare at him. "Right. Us women folk are meek and

sensitive and can't handle getting our hands dirty. We need tough men to do that for us."

Andrea smiles. "I'm sorry, I didn't mean to offend your gender. I was just stating facts as I know them."

"Then you know nothing. The reason most women in our world don't participate is because you men decide we can't handle it."

"I said I'm sorry and I meant it. I was just trying to compliment you and let you know that if you don't want to participate, you don't have to. My men and I can get revenge and answers. You don't have to be there unless you want to."

"I want to," I scowl.

He nods. "Then you shall be."

I start to walk, but my legs give out, and I stumble.

Andrea catches me. "You should eat something. Torturing someone definitely works up an appetite."

Food is the last thing I want, but I nod and let Andrea lead me into the dining room.

He pulls out a chair for me near the end of the table, and I sit before he scoots me in. Then he sits at the head of the table, next to me, as his men fill into the remaining chairs of the long table.

A moment later, his servants are bringing out trays of food. The table is quickly filled with mountains and mountains of food, but all of it makes my stomach curl.

I still haven't taken a pregnancy test, but if my nausea is any indication, I'm definitely knocked up. I can't think about it, especially not now, without breaking into a million little pieces on the floor.

My grief is overwhelming. It's in every fiber of my body. It's a shadow I will always live under. But I can't face it either. Right now, I need to appear strong. I can't break down anymore in front of all these men.

I don't trust Andrea, let alone any of his men. I don't

trust men in general. I know what they are all capable of, and Andrea's intentions with me are still unclear.

I know what my intentions are: revenge.

It's what's going to prevent me from drowning in grief. It will shield me from the pain of the loss. And it will make me appear strong, which I'll need to survive.

"You're not touching your food," Andrea says.

"I'm not hungry—at least, not for food."

"What are you hungry for?"

"Revenge," I say viciously.

Andrea's lips curl up into a sly smile. "Good girl."

"Don't patronize me," I snap.

He chuckles. "I hope I'm worthy of you someday, Rialta Corsi. I know you're grieving and technically still married to that monster in the basement, but soon you'll be free. Soon you'll be ready to move on to new, better man, and I hope I'm that man."

I narrow my eyes. "It's not really my decision, is it? It's my father's. He already passed over you when he selected Lennox; what makes you think he'll pick you now?" I raise my eyebrows at him.

Andrea leans back in his chair, lifting his scotch and rattling the ice around as he takes in my words. If he wants me, he has to know the real me. I'm not a meek princess that will yield to his commands.

"You really think you don't have a say? You think your father makes decisions about your future without considering your wishes?"

"Well, since I was forced to marry a man I hate instead of the love of my life, yea, I do."

"There is so much you don't know, Rialta. So much I want to teach you."

I frown, not understanding, but the man sitting to his

left gets his attention, and the conversation ends. And I'm left without answers.

Knowing I'm going to need sustenance to get through this, I pick at my food while plotting my revenge in my head. I think of all the ways I can hurt him. I could stab him, burn him, mark him, kill him. He deserves to die for what he did. And I know soon enough, it will happen.

But then what?

Will I ever be free?

Will I ever be able to choose?

What happens to me? To this baby?

I'm still destined to die. There are still enemies who want to see the Corsi line dead—that includes this unborn baby. We're all fated to die, and there's no way to stop that.

So does it really matter how I spend my final days? That's what this feels like—the end. Death has been chasing me all my life, and it's finally about to catch up with me. The only thing I have left to do is get revenge.

Andrea pulls out his buzzing phone. I see my father's name, Vincent Corsi, flash on the screen, and I freeze, knowing my future might be decided by this phone call.

"Yes," Andrea answers, showing no respect for my father. That's something I know he won't tolerate.

Andrea listens carefully as the rest of the room is silent.

My heart beats frantically in my chest. *What is Vincent saying?* I have no idea how he's going to react to all of this.

But then Andrea's lips curl up in a wicked smile, and I know the answer before he hangs up. I know what my father has decided before Andrea tells the room, "Vincent has given us permission to kill Lennox."

CHAPTER 3

Lennox

I HEAR FOOTSTEPS—*HER* *footsteps.*

She's still wearing heels, and they click against the floor as she approaches me.

She's alone.

Finally, we're alone.

But I can't lift my head. I can barely open my eyes. My shoulders and wrists are numb from being over my head for so long. Blood oozes down my back. And the pain has overwhelmed my senses to the point that I don't even feel it anymore. I'm not sure I can feel anything anymore.

That is until she walks closer, and my heart flips in my chest. It has a reason to pump again. As it beats, the pain in the rest of my body returns, and I start to fight again, remembering what I'm fighting for: her.

Rialta stops right in front of me.

My heart goes into overdrive, and I hope the blood through my body gives me enough strength to lift my head and look at her. But it's a useless endeavor—I'm too weak.

Suddenly, her fingers thread through my hair, and I gasp. It feels fucking incredible, and it gives me hope.

And then her fingers dig into my scalp, and she grips my hair, yanking my head up until I'm face to face with her. The move is a sharp contrast to the gentle touch she displayed just a second earlier.

Rialta's expression is blank and unreadable, but it doesn't stop me from grinning at her. I can't help it. No matter the reason for her visit, I'm happy that she's here. I get to see her again.

We stare at each other, neither of us speaking. But the longer I study her, the more I realize that she's changed. She's as far as she can get from the girl I first met. The girl I hated. The girl who seemed naive and overly protected. The girl who seemed selfish, incapable of putting others before herself.

I couldn't have been more wrong about her. *But now that I'm in love with her, am I still blinded to her true self?*

Who is Rialta Corsi?

The corner of her lip lifts into a vicious snarl as if reading my mind and answering.

Has she been this wicked, divine creature this whole time?

I rake my teeth over my bottom lip.

"Don't do that," she says.

"Do what?" my voice is soft and joking.

"That," she hisses as I rake my teeth over my bottom lip again.

I chuckle. "Why? What does it make you feel, wifey?"

"Don't call me that. I hate that I have to be married to you."

"Do you now? I'm pretty sure you love being my wife. You love how cruel I can be. And you especially love the things I do to you in bed."

"I hate you. You killed Kit. I'll never love you. I'll always hate you. There is nothing you could do that could ever make me forgive you."

"Hmm."

She glares at me, and that's when I spot the shiny metal in her hand.

"Since when did you learn how to hold a gun?"

She grinds her teeth together. "Wouldn't you like to know."

"Did Andrea teach you?"

She doesn't answer me.

"Did Vincent? Ri? Beckett?"

No answer. She gives me no clues as to who she really is. *Has she known how to hold a gun this hold time? How to use one? Does she know self-defense? Was she just pretending to be a weak princess instead of the fierce woman in front of me? Was she playing me? If so, for what purpose?*

"Vincent said we can kill you now."

My eyes focus again, looking at her face. I'm waiting for the moment she uses that gun to kill me.

She's strong enough to do it.

Maybe she's even killed before.

"You never needed his permission to kill me."

"That's true. The real question is, how long should you suffer before I kill you? You don't seem to be in nearly enough pain. How long did you let Kit suffer before you killed him?" She sniffles, sucking back a sob.

Dammit, why did I kill him? Why can't I remember?

I open my mouth to say I'm sorry but stop. I don't know if I'm sorry. I don't know if I killed Kit for a good reason. My apology is empty without the truth.

I want to comfort her, though. I want to wrap my arms around her and give her the space to cry until she has nothing left inside. I want to get down on my knees and tell her how sorry I am. But most of all, I want to give her vengeance for losing the man she loved.

I know how that feels. I lost a woman I loved. And I'm

losing Rialta now after only just realizing my love for her. I know how important it is to get revenge for losing the most important person to you. Even if she needs to kill me to get that retribution. Growing up a Retribution King taught me that.

"You should get revenge," I say.

She blinks, light from the stairs reflecting off her face in the shadowy darkness of the basement.

"Revenge means you'll be dead," she responds.

"I'm not afraid of death; neither are you. I deserve to die, so kill me. It won't take away all of your pain, but it will help. You'll be able to keep living, keep breathing, if you get retribution for Kit's death."

I take a deep, calming breath trying to blow it out to her to give her calmness and peace with whatever she decides. If I'm to die tonight, I'd rather die by her hand. I'd rather die with just the two of us here. I'd rather die giving her peace than die fighting or getting my own revenge. If my last act on this earth can be giving the woman I love some small sort of tranquility, then I'll die with a purpose.

She doesn't raise her gun. She just stares at me, perplexed, trying to understand what I'm saying.

I don't rush her. I soak every bit of her in. She's still wearing the same dress she wore on our date. I don't know how long it's been—hours, days, weeks—but I wish I could go back to that date. Not to prevent myself from drinking the wine she laced but to tell her the truth faster. It might not have changed the outcome, but at least it would have given her all the facts. She would have known how I felt about her, and she would have known why I've done what I've done. She would have understood why. I probably would have even told her why I killed Kit.

It wouldn't have mattered. I would have still ended up here, being tortured for what I did and eventually killed.

And it wouldn't change how she feels about me. She hates me. She was playing me.

Does that make me hate her?

No.

The truth is I never hated her.

Never.

I grin.

She narrows her eyes in a glare and raises her gun.

I grin wider. When I go, I'll go looking at the most beautiful woman in the world.

She fires.

The bullet whizzes past my head, skimming my hair.

She smirks.

Silently, she turns on her heels and starts walking toward the stairs.

My heart races.

My body aches for her.

Who the hell is Rialta Corsi?

I don't know, but I do know one thing, and I can't keep it inside anymore.

"I love you, Rialta Corsi."

She pauses at the base of the stairs. "And I hate you, Lennox Corsi."

CHAPTER 4

Rialta

I SHUT MY MIND OFF, focusing on the tap of my heels as I walk up the stairs to my bedroom. I pass several of Andrea's men down the red-carpeted hallway with gold-framed paintings on the cream-wallpapered walls. The whole mansion is hideously gaudy. It probably hasn't been updated in decades.

I'm just thankful to have my own suite. It's a large bedroom with a sitting area and an expansive ensuite bathroom.

I shut the door behind me and immediately turn the lock. It won't be enough to keep anyone out. I know that, but it gives me a tiny bit of security.

I'm still gripping the gun I fired at Lennox's head as I walk to the bathroom.

These clothes are suffocating. While I kick off my heels, I set the gun down on the marble counter and unzip my dress. I unhook my bra and push down my panties, finally naked.

I step into the large shower, and only then do I flick the water on. Cool water hits the top of my head, and I shiver. But it numbs me—just what I need—and washes away the sweat and pain for a few seconds before the water turns warm.

I stand under the shower head, letting the water hit me without the energy to wash anything. I'm tired—so fucking tired. I've never felt this tired in my entire life. I don't know if it's from the grief, the pain, or...or possibly being pregnant.

Despite not having a positive test result, I know the truth deep in my bones. I have no idea what I'm going to do.

I'm pregnant with Kit's child.

Kit, who is now dead.

It's the last piece of him I have.

But I don't want to be pregnant. I don't want a child. I've never wanted to be a mother.

And my life is complicated. I don't know who I am or how much time I have left of this life. I've been running from danger for so long that I don't know if I'll even live long enough to birth this child. And if I do live that long, I'll never live long enough to raise the child to adulthood. My child will forever have a target on his or her head until the danger is gone, until I find a way out of this life for all of us.

No, I can't be pregnant.

And yet, I'm exhausted. I could sleep for hours on end. Every smell of food I encounter makes my stomach want to hurl. My boobs are heavy and sore, and I swear they've grown a size or two overnight.

I run my hands up my face and over my hair, trying to wash away the thought. I don't know for sure, not until I test. *And then what?*

I don't know what my next move is. *What do I do with Lennox? What about Andrea? How do I convince my father to let me make my own choices? And even if I could make my own decisions, what would I choose?*

I flip off the water and grab a fluffy white towel hanging

outside the door, wrapping it under my arms before stepping out. I instantly freeze, feeling his presence before I look up.

"Don't you know it's rude to enter a woman's bathroom while she's showering without knocking first?" I snap as I walk to the connected closet Andrea had filled with women's clothes.

I flick through the apparel but realize most of them are a size or two smaller than I actually am. If I am pregnant, nothing will fit for very long with my swelling belly. I grab a stretchy black dress that might still fit. As much as I want to choose a sweatshirt and leggings, I need to feel powerful around Andrea and his men.

When I walk back into the bathroom, Andrea is still leaning against the doorframe with lust-filled eyes.

My skin crawls under his gaze, but I know exactly how I'm going to handle him. I drop the towel and watch his jaw drop as he takes in my naked body. His gaze starts with my breasts and then drops to my legs and everything in between.

Quickly, I grab the gun on the counter and aim it at his heart.

His lips curl into a wicked grin. "Masterful, my darling."

"If you don't want a bullet in your chest, I suggest you go wait in my bedroom and never come into my bedroom or bathroom again without my permission."

He puts his hands up casually, clearly unworried that I'd really shoot him. It makes me want to shoot him just to prove a point. I'm very willing to shoot and kill anyone who crosses me, and I've had enough of being controlled by men.

He exits the bathroom and shuts the door behind him.

I let out a breath, calming myself and setting the gun down on the counter. Keeping an eye on the bathroom door, I get dressed, blow dry my hair, and put on some makeup—forcing Andrea to wait half an hour for me.

I'm impressed that he actually had the patience to wait and not barge in, barking orders at me.

Finally, I strap on some heels and find a purse in the closet for my gun before opening the bathroom door.

Andrea is occupying one of the two chairs in the sitting area. He stands up with a soft smile when he sees me.

"You're worth the wait. You're stunning, Rialta."

I nod, flipping my long, dark hair to the side.

He motions for me to sit in the chair opposite him. I do, holding a confident gaze on Andrea as I walk. His eyes devour the curves of my body in this skintight dress.

We both take a seat.

"Now, what did you come here to discuss?" I ask.

He tilts his head, his eyes still perusing my body and lingering a long time on the swell of my breasts. "Always so down to business with you, baby. I just wanted to talk."

"I'm not your baby, Andrea."

"No, I know you need time. You just lost the man you love. And we haven't killed your husband yet. But I've been in love with you for a long time, Rialta. Soon you'll realize you and I belong together."

I don't argue with him. I'm not sure how I want to proceed. *Do I actually want Andrea, or should I take my chances with the next guy my father will choose for me?*

"I'm not sure I'll ever be ready for a relationship again."

Andrea takes my hand. "You will, baby, you will."

I nod, letting him hold my hand.

"I know you loved Kit, but he wasn't your destiny. You knew that—that's why you married Lennox. Lennox was wrong for you in many ways, but it's a good thing you were only together a short time. It will be easy for you to move on, and your marriage won't even be remembered by anyone in a year's time. There will be no real consequences. He didn't knock you up yet, and..."

I fidget in my seat.

Andrea's eyes are hyper-focused on my reaction to his words.

"Did he hurt you?"

My heart slows, realizing he didn't just figure out I might be pregnant.

"Yes," I mutter.

"I'm going to kill him," Andrea says. He jumps up and paces. "I can't believe the bastard hurt you. I knew he forced the marriage, but I didn't think he would actually hurt you."

I still, watching Andrea get worked up.

"I'm going to kill him. Tonight. That bastard doesn't deserve to live another second."

"No."

Andrea stops pacing and looks at me, concerned. "He has to die for what he did to you. If you grew any feelings for him, it's only because he fucked with your mind, sweetheart. It's not because your feelings are real."

"I know, and I didn't grow any feelings for Lennox."

"Then I'm going to kill him tonight. You will have your revenge, and then you will be able to move on from this terrible nightmare and start your future with me."

"I want to be the one to kill him."

Andrea's eyes widen, and his lips curl again. "You're so strong, baby. You don't have to—"

"I do. I want to be the one to kill him. Promise me you'll let me get my own revenge."

"I promise."

"Tomorrow."

"Why wait?"

"Because tomorrow is, was, Kit's birthday. That's the day I want to kill Lennox."

Andrea swiftly walks to me, grabs my hand, and pulls

me to standing. He plants his lips on mine before I can protest.

"At dawn, you will kill Lennox, and then I'll spend the rest of tomorrow convincing you to be mine." His lips land on mine again in a deep, hungry kiss.

A kiss I get lost in.

A kiss that destroys me.

A kiss that should elicit something strong in me—good or bad.

But I feel nothing.

Andrea pulls back. "How do you want to spend tonight, baby?"

"Teaching Lennox a lesson."

CHAPTER 5

Lennox

SUDDENLY I'M FALLING to the floor of the dungy basement. As I realize the chains holding me up were cut, I don't bother trying to stand or brace for the ground. I can't—I have no strength. I've been beaten, cut, and sliced to within an inch of my life. It's been days since I've had any food or water. My arms have been tied above my head for so long that they're entirely drained of their blood.

I don't even register the impact of the hard dirt floor.

"On your feet," one of Andrea's goons says.

He's an idiot if he thinks I can respond to his command.

"I said on your feet." My body flops over as the toe of his boot kicks me square in the side, flopping my naked body onto my back.

A wheezy groan escapes from my lips.

The man laughs at the state of me.

"Pick him up."

Two sets of arms lift me by my shoulders and drag me up the wooden stairs. My legs bounce on each step, digging wooden splinters into my shins.

I'm completely dead weight, unable to even open my

eyes. I don't bother trying, as I'll need any strength I have for later, I'm sure. I wish Rialta would have killed me earlier. Whatever Andrea has in store for me will not mean a peaceful exit from this world.

They drag me down a hallway and stop to throw me into a wooden chair. They bind my ankles and wrists to the chair, ignoring the futility of the rope. I can't walk; I'm no threat to them.

I should be in immense pain, but my nerves have been so overloaded that I physically can't register pain anymore. Blood covers my naked skin more than my full-body tattoos.

"Lennox, so nice of you to join us," Andrea says.

My head hangs, my eyes are still closed, and I don't move at the sound of his voice. Only one voice is worth my energy in lifting my head.

"Yes, we thought you might want to join us for dinner," Rialta says.

A tender smile spreads across my face as I force my swollen eyelids open to look at her. And I'm not disappointed when I see my girl. She's in a skintight black dress, showing off her curves. Her hair is blow-dried in long waves.

"Stunning," I croak out. I swear she blushes and then quickly gives me a stern look, annoyed she reacted to my compliment.

As much as I want to keep my eyes on her, I can't. My head dips again.

"Help Lennox hold his head up," Andrea barks, and then there are hands on my head holding it up.

"Better," Andrea says. He pulls out a chair for Rialta, and she takes a seat at the small circular table filled with candles and roses in the center.

It's meant to be romantic. It's meant to drive me wild.

I won't let it.

Andrea takes a seat across from her. A steak dinner and

wine is already laid out on the table for them. My mouth salivates at the sight of food.

Even though I can barely think straight, I know this isn't what I was brought up here to observe as they cut into their steaks and make idle talk.

I close my eyes, trying to rest. I try to understand what happened and what's about to happen. But nothing is registering in my battered state.

"There are two ways to end your marriage. Your death…" Andrea says with a vicious smirk. "Which is inevitable, but that would make Rialta a widower—"

"And I'm no widower," Rialta says with a dark tone.

"She deserves a true annulment. She deserves a reason that this marriage was never valid in the first place, so that when she marries me our marriage will be her true marriage, her only marriage," Andrea continues.

I stare at Rialta, my breathing heavy in my chest as I try to figure out how Rialta's feeling. She's a brick wall of emotions. *Is she really this emotionless about what's about to happen? Or is it all a front? Are her emotions hiding beneath the cool exterior and she's just proving how strong I knew she was this entire time?*

Andrea nods, and his men start moving the table and chairs away while Andrea and Rialta stand. She's still holding onto her wine glass, sipping it frequently. *Liquid strength? Or enjoyment?*

Two large black leather chairs are brought in for Andrea and Rialta to sit in, like they are thrones or something.

I gulp, knowing I'll be their entertainment. I'm not sure my body can take anymore.

"Happy annulment day, baby," Andrea says. He might be talking to Rialta, but he's looking at me with a wicked smile. He's going to enjoy what happens next far too much.

My eyes cut to the door as three women strut into the

room. Black high heels adorn their feet, and thin strappy material barely covers their breasts and asses.

My head falls forward. My only salvation is that I can't feel anything. I doubt my body will even react to the women. They can play with my body all they want—it belongs to Rialta. It will only react for her.

The women stop on either side and in front of me. Then my head is lifted by the woman to my left until I'm looking at the woman kneeling between my legs. She has fiery red hair, fake eyelashes, and red lipstick to match her hair.

"I'm sorry," I say, knowing it's all I can do for her. If she's been sold, touched by men, and forced to do worse—there's nothing I can do for her.

She laughs and licks her lips with lust flickering in her eyes. "I'm not—I just wish the goods weren't so damaged so I could enjoy you more."

I close my mouth. At least it's clear she wants this. It somehow makes it easier that no one is forcing her to do this.

I look over her shoulder to where Rialta is sitting and find her still sipping her wine like it's the only thing in the room she can focus on. She wants to stop this but can't. I know her. I love her. She loves me despite all the pain. I probably deserve all the pain, but I'm still sorry.

Sorry for what I've put her through.

Sorry that she's being forced to watch another woman touch me.

Sorry that I can't protect her.

"I'm sorry," I say, looking at Rialta, knowing it doesn't come close to the apology she deserves.

And then I feel the redhead's hand on my dick.

So all my nerve endings aren't completely fried—fuck.

I wish I could say I don't feel the woman's hand stroking up and down my shaft, pulling blood into the only part of my body that has managed not to go numb, but I feel it. The smooth pressure of her hand and the tingling starting in my balls and running through me as she strokes me.

But I'm also tired and wiped out. And while I'm growing hard under her touch, it's a slow process. Even with the women on either side kissing my ears, neck, and lips, my body is taking a long time to respond. The longer it takes, the more tired I become.

I close my eyes, knowing I have no choice but to sleep through it. I wish I could stay strong for Rialta. I wish I could show her that I only have desire for her, but it's probably better for her to see me as a corpse instead of her previous lover.

"Inject him," Andrea says.

"No," I whisper, but it manages to get trapped in the back of my throat.

One of Andrea's men walks forward. My head is jerked to one side, and the sharp pierce of a needle roughly punctures my neck before cool liquid fills my veins.

He releases my head abruptly, and the women stop their groping. Their stares never leave me, though. The room is quiet—watching, waiting for something to happen.

Tick, tock, tick, tock…

One breath, two, three…

Maybe…it won't work.

Maybe whatever drug he injected me with won't have the intended effect on me.

My eyelids are heavy and close with a thud. My head hangs, and I'm pretty sure a snore escapes. I'm two seconds away from falling asleep naked in this chair when my head jolts upright.

I snarl at the man that jerked my head up as my neck aches from the whiplash, but there is no man there. The cool liquid turns to warm as it races through my body. I pull at the ropes binding me to the chair, desperate to break free. My skin crawls with fierce hotness I can't explain, and I have this intense desire to jump up, start running, and never stop. I feel like I could run an entire marathon and not even break a sweat.

What the fuck did the monster inject me with?

I find Andrea across the room, and I know what he did. The amused look on his face tells me exactly what's about to happen. I may be a dead man, but I'm going to find a way to kill him.

And then I feel their hands on me.

I don't even have time to suck in a breath before the rage takes over, and I'm pulling with a hulk-like strength to get out of the bindings. I need away from their touch. They can't touch me. They have no right. I belong to Rialta. I'm hers, only hers.

But the grip on my cock tightens, sliding up and down my slick shaft, and kisses pepper my jawline from each side as hands slide up and down my pecs and abs.

I glare at Andrea—focusing all of my rage on him. I need the fury to keep me grounded and to give me enough strength to break free.

I can't focus on what they are doing to me. And I sure as hell can't look at Rialta. I need to stay in control. I don't want to let my body take over. I don't want to feel this...

Blood rushes into my cock like a waterfall. One whoosh of blood and my cock is rock hard in this woman's hand. And it's the most fucking painful thing.

I slam my body up and down, determined to escape. I need to stop the pleasure in my cock beginning to roll up and down my body.

I don't want this. I refuse to feel anything.

Hands slam down on my shoulders, holding me in place.

I can't move. I'm glued to the chair. The adrenaline

coursing through me isn't enough to overcome the weakened state my body is in. If only my cock would listen. If only it was broken along with the rest of my body.

I try to focus on Andrea, on my hatred, on my revenge. But I'm not strong enough.

The roiling of pleasure after so much pain feels euphoric. All I want to do is let go and enjoy it.

But Rialta is here.

I love her.

I only have hours, maybe only minutes, left on this earth, and I'm not going to spend them breaking my vow of love for her. I've betrayed her enough.

Pleasure curls in my belly as a mouth wets the tip of my cock and a tongue swooshes over it. I bite down on my tongue until I taste blood to keep from letting a single moan of pleasure out. I'll suffer in pain instead of enjoying this. I will not cause Rialta any more pain. I refuse.

Andrea's grin widens as he sees the torment I'm in. And the bastard knows exactly what to do to make it worse. He grabs Rialta, pulling her under his arm and into my line of sight.

She's so beautiful.

No, don't think about her.

Don't...

But it's too late.

My dick is rock hard, aching for a release. And my throat can't contain my groans of pleasure anymore.

It pours out of me all at once—the groan, along with spurts of cum in long ribbons onto the woman's hand between my thighs.

I'm panting hard, my body shaking from a mix of adrenaline and aftershock from my orgasm. I search for Rialta, but she's no longer under Andrea's arm. *Where did she go?*

She hates me even more than before—I'm sure of it.

This feels worse than anything I've done to her. I've had horrible things done to me—there's a reason I am the way I am. The only reason I can do horrible things myself is because of what I've gone through. Pain isn't new to me. Feeling broken is how I live my life. Last time I went through this I lost the love of my life.

I won't do that again.

When I die, I'm going to die loving Rialta. I'm going to die with hope that she can live a better life.

The women leave me now that they've fulfilled their mission.

I frantically search the room. *Where is Rialta? Did she leave? Was it all too much for her?*

Andrea chuckles as if this is all a game to him. He's enjoying every second of my misery.

I fight against the restraints again. My chair bounces on the ground but doesn't break. There might have been a time that I could have broken free, but my muscles have deteriorated to nothing. Even with the adrenaline coursing through me I don't have the strength to break the flimsy chair or slip my wrists or ankles from the rope binding me. I'm fucking useless to protect Rialta, and my instincts scream that I need to protect her.

"Hold still, you're not going to want to miss this," Andrea says as two guards hold me down in the chair again.

Metal bars are brought in with leather straps dangling between them, and my stomach drops.

No...no, no, no.

I buck hard, but the guards keep me in place with barely a push of their hands on my shoulders.

"My dear, are you ready?" Andrea asks in a sickeningly sweet tone.

"Yes," Rialta says from the doorway.

My eyes cut to her in an instant. Her hard nipples are

puckering against the black lace lingerie with crotchless panties she's now wearing. Black heels adorn her feet, her hair is brushed over to one side, and her makeup has been thickened.

She's any man's dream—so goddamn sexy. But she's mine, not his.

"I have a special treat for you, baby. I know how much you like being tied up, so I thought you'd enjoy my custom swing," Andrea says, holding his arm out to proudly display the sex swing in the center of the room.

Her lips curl up. "That was so considerate of you."

There's no fear there, no signs that this is all an act or that she doesn't want to do this.

My heart stops as she walks over to the swing where Andrea is standing.

"Lennox cheated on you, so your marriage can now be annulled," Andrea says as he licks his lips.

"Good. I'm no longer Lennox's."

"Whose are you?"

"I belong to no man." Her teeth scrape over her bottom lip. "But if you get me pregnant, I'll be yours forever."

CHAPTER 6

Lennox

ANDREA WON'T BE GETTING her pregnant. I won't let him. He won't be fucking her or even touching her. It's an act, I know it is. I don't know why she's going along with it so convincingly, but I know she doesn't want him to fuck her.

Rialta may hate me, but she loved Kit. And she wouldn't want to be with another man so soon after Kit's death. *What's her endgame?*

She flashes me a sinful glare.

Unless...she hates me so much that she's willing to fuck him to get back at me?

I swallow hard.

No.

She wouldn't. She doesn't hate me that much. And she respects herself too much to be touched if she doesn't want it.

I grit my teeth together and wait. I wait for her to make her move because she has to have a move to get out of this situation. *What dirt does she have on Andrea that will make him stop? Will she overpower him when he's vulnerable?*

Either way, I'd bet my life on her.

I implore myself to be patient and wait for her to enact her plan.

She walks closer to the swing with all the confidence in the world. Every eyeball and dick in the room are straining in her direction. She bats her eyes at one of the guards in charge of making sure I stay in my chair.

Andrea growls. "Everyone out."

I smirk. Apparently, he doesn't like sharing her now that she's agreed to be his.

The guards file out, a couple of them flashing one last longing look in my wife's direction. I will not stop calling her mine until I hear from her own lips away from this place that she no longer wants to be my wife. Me being forced to come doesn't annul our marriage, and neither does her fucking Andrea now. The only thing that will end our marriage is her word.

Andrea holds out his hand, and she immediately places hers in his. A sly grin spreads across his crooked face. His dark eyes intensify with lust and revenge.

Then he grabs her by the waist and lifts her up. She grabs onto the bindings behind her, slipping her wrists through the loops, while he lifts her legs. She slips them through the loops, sliding them up her thighs, followed by another loop at her feet.

"Spread your legs for me and show me how beautiful your pussy is," Andrea says, stepping back from between her legs as she spreads them wider, giving me as clear a view of her body as he has.

I gasp at the sight of her. She's so fucking perfect. I never realized how much I like BDSM until she came into my life, but now all I want is to tie her up in my bedroom for hours. I want to paint her ass red and mark every inch of her body as mine.

"Do you see what you lost, Lennox? She was yours, and you had to be selfish. You killed the man she loved instead of giving her the world," Andrea says.

I don't respond to him. I don't let him bait me. I know what I lost. I lost the love of my life.

Rialta's eyes grow heavy, and her cheeks pinken. "Baby, come here. I need you." Her raspy voice sets me on edge.

Andrea steps closer to her, and I hold my breath, anxious to see how far she's going to let him go before dropping the bomb on him. He moves between her legs, kneeling between them and dropping his lips to her pussy.

Stop it, I implore her. *Don't let him touch you.*

Her gaze meets mine, and I know she can read my mind in this moment. Then Andrea's head angles down as Rialta's head drops back, and Andrea takes her into his mouth.

No.

Andrea grips her thighs, keeping them spread as he devours her pussy with his mouth, rocking her body back and forth in the swing against his lips.

I can't see Rialta's face as her head has fallen back. *Is she enjoying herself and can't look at me while she does this?*

She's going to stop this. She's not going to let him go further than licking her. This is all going to end. She's gotten her revenge on me. She's not going to destroy herself to hurt me any further.

A moan vibrates around the room—her moan.

My ears burn with that moan. It's the same moan she made when I fucked her. It's as genuine as it gets. It wasn't strangled, holding back her pleasure like mine when they pulled an orgasm from me. This is her letting herself feel everything, maybe even wanting it.

"I'm so close," she moans as Andrea rocks her against his mouth.

"Yes, baby, come."

"No, I want you inside me when I come."

My world stops at her words. This is it. The moment of truth. She could stop this. She could at least attempt to stop it. And if she tried, I would find the strength to help. I know I would. I'd break free. I just need her to give me the signal.

Unless she really wants this—wants him?

I've seen them grow closer. Maybe she even knew him from before. I don't know, but I'm about to get answers.

Andrea stands, happy to oblige to her request.

Rialta pulls her head back up and looks me dead in the eyes. Andrea undoes his pants and pulls out his hard cock.

I love you, I mouth to her. *Let me help you. Don't do this.*

There's a dangerous gleam in her eyes that turns to lust.

She wants this. She's not going to stop him.

A rage of pain like nothing I've ever felt before rips through me at the same time Rialta spreads her legs, and Andrea drives inside her in one thrust. The look of pleasure on her face, combined with her guttural moan, fills my ears.

My body moves without thinking. I need to stop this. I need to help her. I need to prove that she's still mine, that I never meant to hurt her. That if I killed Kit, it was for a very good reason, not to hurt her. I love her. And I'm pretty sure she loves me too deep down beneath the need for revenge.

But I lost her.

Rialta's not mine.

She's his.

She doesn't love me.

She hates me.

But even as I think the words, I don't fully believe them. Even though I'm watching her be fucked by another man, I don't truly believe that she's really gone. I can fix this if she'd only listen to me. I don't care how many other men she fucks; I'll always love her.

Andrea slides his cock deeper into her, grabbing onto

her ass in the swing as he slams her body into his again and again and again, driving me mad each time.

I roar with anger at him touching her. She's my fucking wife, and he's turned her against me. I don't care that he's winning. I don't care that he's getting off on my pain—that they both are.

Rialta looks at me again, eyes glazed over, telling me how much she's enjoying this and is about to come on his dick.

I feel the rage building. I'm so close to breaking everything.

"Come in me, Andrea. I want all your cum. I want you to get me pregnant, so my father will have no choice but to let me marry you."

Her words are like a death sentence to me.

I explode—breaking all the bindings in one swoop.

She screams out her orgasm as Andrea grunts and groans, getting closer and closer to his.

He doesn't notice that I'm free.

He doesn't know that I'm about to kill him.

He doesn't know...

I feel a sharp stab in the neck and then darkness coming for me again. But no darkness can compare to the pain that's already in my heart. I don't know if this is the end, if death has finally caught up to me, but whatever this darkness is I welcome it.

CHAPTER 7

Lennox

MY EYES SHOOT OPEN, but darkness still surrounds me. Yet it's a new type of darkness—flickers of moonlight shine through the window, rattling against my head as the car bounces down a bumpy road.

I'm in a car.

I'm not dead.

And I'm in the front passenger's seat. I don't know if my driver knows I'm awake yet. I don't know if there is a man in the back with a gun pointed at my head. But I do know this might be my only chance.

I lunge for the driver, intent on taking him out quickly with my bare hands if I have to.

I grab his throat and immediately tighten my grip. Sucking the life out of this man seems like a kind way for him to go considering who he works for and what's currently happening to my wife. He deserves to be tortured and then slowly killed.

An elbow pops me in the nose hard as the car swerves, but I don't let go. I won't be able to kill them all, but at least I can get this one. His fist hits me again, knocking me back.

"Lennox, it's me, Hayes—what the fuck, man?"

Hayes.

I blink slowly, taking in his long hair, square glasses, and green eyes.

It's Hayes.

This isn't a trick.

He's really here.

I grab him again.

Hayes winces away, afraid I'm going to try to strangle him again. But when I wrap my arms around him in an embrace, he takes a slow breath and wraps one of his arms around me too.

"You're safe," he says.

I nod. "Thank you for rescuing me."

"Of course. We'd do anything for you."

"We?"

I look to the backseat but find it empty. Hayes picks up speed, and I realize we are far from safe based on how quickly he's driving. But I'm as safe as I can ever be.

Then my memory suddenly hits me.

"We have to go back."

Hayes doesn't take his eyes off the road. "No, we don't."

"We do. We have to rescue Rialta."

His grip on the wheel tightens until I see the white of his knuckles. "We don't," he says, calmer.

"She's my wife! We have to save her!"

Hayes rolls his shoulders back. "She is safe. She was never in any danger."

"You don't know that! It could have all been an act. She—"

"She was playing us. The whole time. We have evidence that she and Andrea have been planning this. She was in love with him and wanted to marry him, not Kit, from the get-go. But they knew Vincent would never agree. She went along with her father's plan and then made Andrea the hero so her father would agree he's the best choice."

I shake my head, not believing it. Hayes was Rialta's biggest supporter. He knows her almost as well as I do, but I still don't believe it.

"Either way, we need to get her. She's the only way we learn the truth and save ourselves."

Hayes pauses before answering. "We have her."

"What does that mean?" my voice snaps.

"It means that when we rescued you, we got her out as well."

"Where is she?"

"Beckett and Gage took her back in the other car."

I frown.

"Take me to her," I growl.

Hayes doesn't argue. He also doesn't say anything else for the rest of the drive.

About an hour later, Hayes slows to a normal speed, and his shoulders begin to relax. He's no longer worried about who's following us, and we're close.

"How are you feeling?" he asks.

Like every fucking bump in the road makes my head want to explode in pain. But I don't say that; it's nothing compared to my worry about my wife.

I glare at him instead.

He tosses some pain pills at me, and I swallow them dry, not asking any questions. My wounds and injuries need tending too, but that will have to wait. Hayes didn't even attempt to dress me; he just tossed a blanket around me. I don't give a damn that I'm still naked, still bleeding. My entire body feels like it's on fire; not one part of me was spared. And I haven't even let the darkness of being violated by that woman or what Rialta did into my brain.

Pain is not an emotion; it's a weakness. It's a silly gut

check to let you know your body isn't functioning at optimal levels. You might die if you don't do something soon. Pain isn't helpful to me—I already know my body isn't functioning at optimal levels, and every second of every day I'm closer to death.

But Rialta—I need her to live.

Finally, Hayes takes a turn into an underground garage, and I know we're in whatever safe house they have commandeered. Hayes turns sharply into a parking spot, and I jump out before he's even slammed on the breaks.

I hobble to Gage's car, not having any of the adrenaline left in my body to do more. I throw open the back door, but the empty seat isn't even warm. They've gotten here long before us.

"Where is she?" I turn to Hayes with venom in my eyes.

"Come on," he says solemnly.

I grab his shirt threateningly, but I'm sure it looks like a small puppy scratching at his throat. That's the amount of threat I am to him in my current condition.

"Help me."

Hayes sighs.

"Help her," I beg.

He stares at me deeply, like he's not sure who he should trust or what he should say. It's so unlike Hayes to be carrying pain with him. He's usually so carefree and full of life. He never lets the darkness in, but he's carrying it now.

Finally, he nods.

That's all I get from him. Not a real confirmation. Not an, *I'll do whatever you need* or *I'll lay down my life like I did before to save her.* Nothing of the sort, just a simple nod of the head.

But my life depends on that nod.

Hayes leads me into the elevator after tossing me the blanket I left in the car back. I know it's not for modesty reasons. I'm guessing he thinks my body needs every drop of warmth it can take to survive until he can get me medical help.

He hits the top floor, and up we go. Floor after floor my heart pounds in my chest, throbbing to be near her.

I need her. Once I see her alive, and well, then I can collapse. Then I can heal. But first, her.

The doors open, and Hayes leads me to another door at the end of a long hallway.

He knocks.

Second after second passes by in agony. She's on the other side of this door. I can finally talk to her—get some answers. I can finally hold her. I can tell her I love her—that she's mine and I'm hers. That I could never hate her. I can ask for her forgiveness. I can—

The door opens.

Gage is standing inside the entryway looking at me with a soft expression, just as unlike him as Hayes. Gage is usually all business—but this expression says *I'm sorry, man, there was nothing I could do.*

No.

I don't know if I speak the word out loud or not, but I push past him—a brick of a man I shouldn't be able to move in my condition, but I push him out of the way like he's nothing more than a fly I'm swatting out of my face.

The apartment is big. Too many rooms and doors.

She screams, and my heart stops.

It's high-pitched and dripping in a sharp piercing of pain. She's not rolling in agony from something that Andrea did. She's not moaning from some doctor trying to heal her. This is a fresh sound of new pain being inflicted.

I run. Even though I don't have any strength or energy in my body to make my muscles move, I'm suddenly full of energy. I get to the door at the end of the hallway where her screams came from. I grab the door handle, but it's locked.

I hear Hayes and Gage behind me. If they make it to me before I get through the door, they'll probably drag me away, maybe even drug me.

I kick the door with everything I have, knocking the cheap lock open just as Rialta screams again.

I'm going to murder whoever is hurting her. But then I see her.

Her wrists are bound together with rope, yanked above her head, and secured to the post behind her. She's slumped on the floor, and there's a cut across her cheek and another on the underside of her arm.

Knife wounds.

My eyes flick to the man holding the knife, the man hurting my wife.

Beckett.

I thought he was my friend. He's a man I've saved and protected—risking my own life to do so. But I don't care who he was to me; he's a dead man now.

I don't have a gun, a weapon, or enough blood in my body to keep me alive much longer. He has a knife and most likely a gun, but I'm intent on killing him.

Until I see Beckett's face. His is as murderous as mine, but my brain can't process why. All I see is red.

Rialta whimpers, bringing my attention back to her and away from Beckett.

She's in pain, and I'm going to stop this right now. I need my hands on her more than I need to kill Beckett.

"Knife," I say, holding out my hand to Beckett.

I don't know what he's going to do. I don't know why we both want to kill each other. But I hope that everything we've been through will keep him from doing something stupid.

He hesitates, not moving.

"She's my wife," I growl.

Beckett looks at me, really looks, like he's trying to understand me. Whatever he sees looks like disappointment. He shakes his head in refusal. I guess we are going to have this fight after all.

But then he hands me the knife.

I turn and rush to Rialta, beginning to saw apart the ropes binding her.

She doesn't say anything.

I don't either.

Finally, the last of the ropes come loose, and I pull her wrists free.

Our eyes connect in uncertainty. Neither of us knows who the other is any more or where we stand with each other. All I know is I love her. I was wrong before. She's my soulmate, and just looking at her is like looking into heaven.

I scoop her into my arms.

"Lennox, you shouldn't—" she starts.

I glare at her, and she shuts up as I lift her. I don't know where I'm taking her, just that I'm going to find somewhere safe.

Beckett steps in front of the open doorway.

"Move," I growl.

He looks from me to her with venom in his eyes. Upon closer inspection, I see the venom is hiding tears threatening to escape.

I hold my breath, knowing the next words that leave his mouth are going to fucking hurt.

"Take her wherever you want. I can't stand the sight of her anymore. Do what you want with her; I won't stop you. But know who she is."

"I know who she is—she's my wife. And I love her."

Beckett nods sadly. "And Ri is my wife. And Rialta and

Andrea took her. They kidnapped her—using her as a hostage in case we were to fuck with their plans."

Beckett pauses. "You fell in love with the devil. And you're going to have to face the consequences, but I'm not going to let her destroy my family."

CHAPTER 8

Rialta

LENNOX DOESN'T RESPOND or react to Beckett's words. He just walks through the open door, still carrying me bride style, even though I know he's hurting. I'm rubbing against raw wounds on his chest, and he's still naked. He's still detoxing from the drugs in his system, still dealing with being violated himself.

He should be passed out and high on painkillers right now while a doctor tends to him, not carrying me. Still, he struts down the hallway as if he had the strength to run a marathon with me in his arms.

We meet Hayes and Gage at the end of the hallway, and they stare at us in surprise. But I see no softness in either of their gazes. They both think I'm a monster, and I am.

"Move," Lennox says firmly, barking the order to them.

But neither of them step aside.

"I'm taking her somewhere safe, and there's nothing either of you can do. Now move if you want to live," Lennox growls.

Gage bites his bottom lip, holding back words. He turns

to Hayes instead. "I'm going back to doing surveillance on Andrea so we can make a plan to get Ri back."

And then Gage leaves us. Hayes stays, looking at us both with tenderness. He's the one with the heart. But I can see that although he and I used to be great friends, his friendship with Ri far outranks me. He's seen my true colors. He knows who I am now. If Beckett hadn't wanted to torture me himself, Hayes would have done it.

"This apartment is safe," Hayes says with the calming voice of a hostage negotiator.

"It's not safe. Beckett tried to kill my wife. Gage wants to kill her too. And you —"

"Don't want to kill anyone," Hayes says.

"I don't believe you."

Hayes steps aside and motions to the other side of the apartment. "Pick any room over there and stay as long as you need. I'll personally stand guard in the hallway to ensure no harm comes to her."

His eyes flick to mine, and to his credit, he hides his disgust with me well. But I know the truth—he hates me. They all do, and with good reason.

"No—" Lennox starts.

"You don't have a choice but to accept my offer. You don't have the strength to find another place to stay. Andrea will come for her, and he'll succeed."

Lennox opens his mouth but stops.

"I'm a man of my word. I don't like Rialta very much at the moment, but I respect that you need to find out the truth for yourself, Lennox. She's your wife, and you need to come to your own conclusion about what you do with her. And Rialta is strong, so no amount of torture is going to get her to tell us where Ri is. Our only hope of getting Ri back is to keep Rialta alive and make a trade with Andrea. You won't be willing to do that until you two have it out."

Hayes glares at me, and I at him.

Lennox doesn't say anything as he carries me down the hallway to the farthest room. He flicks the light on, slams the door shut behind us, and then turns the lock.

We stare at the room. A small queen bed, a bedside table, and a heavy dresser are the only items in the room. There's nothing on the wall, making it feel cold and small, despite the ensuite bathroom.

Lennox doesn't put me down as he walks to the dresser and begins pushing it with his back.

He hisses as the wood hits his open wounds, but I don't say anything. He's a stubborn ass. Me telling him to let me help him won't make a difference. Eventually, he aligns the dresser in front of the door.

It's not much protection, but it would bide us time if someone tried to enter.

Then Lennox carries me to the bathroom, still never putting me down despite the pain he must be in. *I wonder if he thinks I'll run if he puts me down? Or if I'll say something that will make him truly hate me? Something that will make him realize that our marriage is over?*

There's a medicine cabinet that Lennox flips open as he struggles to hold me with his other arm.

I don't offer to help him, and he doesn't ask.

He finds a first aid kit, and then he stomps off, barely keeping me in his arms, until he reaches the bed, where he collapses with me barely contained in his arms.

He quickly scurries off me, grabbing the first aid kit. He opens it and begins throwing items out on the bed as he digs through it. I assume he's looking to cover his wounds so that he doesn't bleed out or get infected.

We don't make eye contact.

We don't speak.

I'm not sure what to say, and neither of us can stand looking into each other's eyes at the moment.

And then Lennox is hovering over me as I lay on my back on the scratchy comforter. He still doesn't meet my gaze as he studies the slice across my cheek. Without a word, he smears some ointment on it and covers it with a small bandage.

He then moves, focusing on his work to the cut under my arm. He bandages my wound there too.

"Are you hurt anywhere else?" His voice is deep, but it doesn't hide his fear. I'm not sure how he wants me to answer. That I was hurt by Andrea or that I wasn't. I think either answer I give is going to hurt him.

So I say nothing.

I sit up, forcing Lennox to stand off me.

He keeps his gaze high, off my body, like he can't stand to look at me. I'm still wearing black lace lingerie with crotchless panties. Lennox could see my entire body if he wanted to, and I find myself missing his wicked gaze on my body.

But he's not mine anymore.

"Your turn," I say, reaching for the first aid kit. He needs more medical attention than what's here, but he won't get help until he's gotten answers out of me.

He shakes his head. "I'm fine."

"You're not fine." I stare at his naked body covered in blood, sweat, and bruises. There isn't an inch of his skin that isn't marked in more than just his usual tattoos. He'll never be the same after what happened.

I don't understand why I'm not tied to a bed. Why he's not torturing me, threatening to kill me for what I've done. He should hate me, but it's clear that he's never been more in love with me.

"Don't act like you care if I live. You'd much prefer I died. You've made that perfectly clear," he says.

"And you've made it clear that you love me, and you'd rather die loving me than let me go and get to live. You're a fool!"

He grins.

"Why the fuck are you grinning?"

He bites his lip as his smile curls wider, and his eyes light up. "Doesn't matter."

I shake my head and huff. "I think you have brain damage; it's the only explanation."

"You're a liar."

I glare at him.

He snarls back with a smirk that says he knows the truth. But he doesn't. No one does. No one knows my true motives. No one knows my truth. Not him. Not Hayes, Gage, or Beckett. Not Andrea. Not my father. No one. And I plan on keeping it that way.

Neither of us blink as we stare each other down. Waiting for the other to speak and reveal all our secrets.

Lennox finally blinks, surrendering.

"But you're not going to tell me who you're lying to, are you? Is it me? Andrea? Yourself?"

I don't react, but he doesn't expect me to.

"So why am I here? And what are you going to do with me if you don't think you're going to get me to talk?" I ask.

He runs his hand through his hair and chuckles. "I honestly don't know what we do next."

It makes me smile, the softest, most genuine reaction I've had in a long time. It makes me ache for things to have been different. For my life to have been my own. For me to have met Lennox in a different life, in a different world. Maybe then we would have dated, fallen in love, gotten married, and started a family. Maybe we would have gotten a happily ever after.

My smile drops.

Lennox frowns at the sight.

"I don't know all the ways you've been hurt—just that you have. By Andrea. By Beckett. By others. By me. You've been hurt too many times. You've lost any man you thought of loving. You've had your future taken from you over and over again. Been told who to marry, who to have babies with."

He pauses, exasperated. "I want answers. I want the truth. And I want to share mine with you. But tonight isn't the night. We both need rest. And I need a doctor if I'm going to survive long enough to convince you to trust me."

His gaze finally rakes up and down my body. He starts at my bare thighs, letting his eyes rest on the slit of fabric between my legs, over the lace on my stomach, then resting on my nipples. His desire grows, causing my nipples to harden. I know he notices. I know he knows what his gaze does to my body.

But I also know he saw how my body reacted to Andrea.

He doesn't know who I love and who I hate.

He doesn't know my endgame any more than I know his.

But damn him for knowing how to turn me on without even touching me. I'm wet between my legs, and desire builds within my core. I'm aching and needy. If Lennox asked, I don't think I could help but say yes.

Lennox's tongue laps over his teeth.

Fuck.

I'm about to open my mouth to tell him to fuck me when I see his legs shake. He can barely even stand on his own two legs much longer.

So I cross my arms across my chest as sense floods back

into me. "I'm not your wife—not any longer. My father won't let our marriage stand after what you did to me. And I'll never forgive you."

"I love you," he says so softly and tenderly. It's not a game. It's not a lie.

"And I love *him*," I say.

"He's dead. I'm sorry, but loving him won't bring him back. I should know."

"That's not who I was talking about," I spit back.

His eyes widen as if I'm confirming his worst fears. But he can't stand much longer. He needs help. And so this conversation will have to continue another time.

"You don't love Andrea."

I don't say anything. There is nothing left to be said.

"I won't let anyone hurt you. Sleep, Rialta. You're safe." Lennox pushes the dresser far enough for him to slip through the door.

I get out of bed and immediately push the dresser back in front of the door.

I'm safe, Lennox says. I'm not. I never will be. And I'm not sure I want to live a safe life anyway. Safe is boring. Safe doesn't get me what I want. Safe doesn't give me a reason to live.

CHAPTER 9

Lennox

"YOU SHOULD REST LONGER," Hayes says as I walk past him in the hallway.

I managed to get a couple of hours of sleep on the other side of Rialta's door, and I need coffee before I talk to her. Luckily, there's a pot already made when I get to the kitchen.

"And ideally, you should be sleeping in a bed. I told you I'd protect Rialta—"

"Like you did before!" I snap at him. "You didn't protect her from Beckett. He would have killed her, and you would have let him."

Hayes has the decency to look guilty. "I wouldn't have let it get that far. Neither would have Gage. And you know Beckett. He has history with Rialta. He wouldn't have killed her. He knows Ri would have murdered him if he killed her sister, even to get her back."

"It doesn't matter. I don't trust you anymore." I turn toward the door.

"I don't trust anyone," I whisper as I stare at Rialta's bedroom door. I can't even trust the woman I love.

"I know, and I'm sorry. I had to choose between two of my best friends, and I was always going to end up hurting someone. I thought Rialta would tell Beckett how to get Ri back, and that would be the end of it. I didn't think he'd have to hurt her. I don't know what's going on with Rialta, but I know that you love her for real. And now that I know that, I will protect her—just as I protect Ri and everyone else here," Hayes says.

I shake my head. There is nothing he can say that will make me feel better.

"I owe you. I'll make it up to you. And it starts with protecting her with my life." Hayes puts his hand on the door. "I'll make sure no one hurts her. Go sleep in a real bed. You let our doctor dress your wounds and give you some meds, but you're never going to heal if you don't rest."

"No, I've rested long enough." Three hours of sleep on the floor outside her room isn't enough, but it's all the time I'll allow myself. I need answers. "Beckett isn't the only one who wants to find Ri and her unborn baby. The longer this goes on, the more we risk getting her back unscathed. I may hate Beckett right now, but I'm still going to do everything I can to save his wife."

Hayes sighs and nods. "Do what you must."

I study him. He wants me to trust him again. And I do —he's seen me through the worst, but I'm still fucking mad at him, and he knows that. He'll do whatever it takes to restore our relationship.

I keep that in mind as I open the door a crack before it hits the dresser.

I grin. Rialta moved it back in front of the door.

"Rialta," I whisper.

I wait.

I'm not sure she's going to wake up, or if she does, move the dresser out of the way.

Just when I'm about to give up and force myself inside, I hear her moving the dresser. I step inside the still dark bedroom. The sun hasn't risen yet, but it will soon enough. And Ri needs to be back before it does.

I reach for the lights and flick them on. I'm stunned to find her still in her black lace lingerie, looking like my goddamn dream woman. I won't be able to think about anything other than fucking her until she tells me she's mine.

"Not fair for you to stare at my body when I don't get to look at yours," she says, staring at the clothes I put on.

"Then maybe you should put something else on."

She looks around the room. "What exactly was I supposed to put on? There aren't any clothes in here."

I groan. I'm an idiot. I can't even remember to provide clothes for her.

I remove my shirt, achingly slow as the fabric brushes over the bandages covering my wounds on my back. Every movement hurts. Every touch against the bandages, no matter how soft, is agony.

She notices. "I'm fine. I don't need—"

I hand her my shirt. "Put it on."

She does. I'm surprised she complied so easily.

"Talk to me," I try another command.

"I'm not a dog you can bark orders at and who'll obey as long as you give me a treat."

My insides warm. "There's my sassy wife. I thought you were gone."

"I'm not your wife."

"Right, you and Andrea took care of that. So what? We're divorced now?"

"Until I kill you."

I nod slowly. "Right. Well, here I am—kill away."

She snarls at me, and I grin. "What, love me too much to kill me?"

"Since I don't have a weapon, it would be kind of hard to kill you."

I shake my head. "Liar. You've made it clear your skills are far greater than you let on. And you're pissed—there's nothing that will stop you when you're angry. You could kill me with your bare hands, but you don't want to."

"You killed Kit—I want to kill you for that."

I sigh. I should have asked Hayes about why I killed Kit before I started this conversation. But I didn't—probably because I don't want to know the truth. I'm a monster, and she deserves to hate me.

"If you hate me for that, then there's no way you fell in love with Andrea so quickly."

She doesn't answer.

"Why him?"

She looks up with wetness in her eyes. "Andrea didn't kill the love of my life."

"That's a reason to not hate him, not to love him. Not to let him fuck you and enjoy it."

The wetness in her eyes glistens as a fire begins to burn. "Who I fuck and what I enjoy is up to me, not you."

"I'm your husband."

"Not anymore. I enjoyed fucking Andrea because I like him; maybe I'm even falling for him. He saved me when I needed him. He helped me get through the worst days of my life. He's strong—he'd be a good Corsi leader, and he's hot. So yes, I enjoyed it."

I growl, but I can't tell if what she's saying is the truth or not.

"Besides all of that, I wanted to decide my own future. My father won't have a choice but to accept Andrea as my husband once he realizes I'm pregnant with Andrea's baby."

My eyes bulge. "You're not pregnant with Andrea's baby. If you're pregnant with anyone's baby, it's mine. But you're not pregnant. And you didn't fuck Andrea until tonight, so even if you are pregnant with his baby, you won't know for a while." I'm sure they weren't fucking behind my back.

She shrugs. "We'll see."

I sigh. "This is getting us nowhere."

"We need to discuss River," she says.

"Do you know where she is?"

Rialta frowns. "No."

I watch her closely. I believe her, but I've been fooled before. I don't trust my own instincts. But this is her sister we're talking about. They share a connection far greater than anything I have with Hayes or Gage or Beckett. Rialta and Ri have protected each other countless times. She may not love me, but she loves her. She wouldn't ever do anything to hurt her.

"But I know how you can get her back," she continues.

"How?"

"Trade me for River."

My lips drop. "No."

She chuckles. "Why not? It's what everyone wants. Andrea wants me back. He doesn't want to hurt my pregnant sister. Beckett, Gage, Hayes—they all want her back. You want her back. And I—"

"No, you don't want to go back to him."

"I want to be with Andrea, not you."

I study every feature of her face. Her pupils are locked on mine and still the same shade of dark brown. They don't dilate or look away, as if she's hiding something. Her lips are soft. Her cheeks are the same shade of pink as always. Her hands don't tremble. Her legs don't shake. She's not looking at me with any desire or lust or fear. There's nothing to show me how she really feels.

My brain flutters back to earlier, when she seemed to willingly let Andrea fuck her.

Fuck.

She could be pregnant with his baby. If she is, no matter what she wants, Vincent and the others will force her to stay with him.

"I love Andrea," she says.

My eyes flick back to her in harsh realization.

"I shouldn't." She sounds ashamed. "But I do. I loved Kit, and now I love Andrea. We bonded in the moments when I was grieving. When he let me get my revenge. When he taught me how to use a gun—how to fight back." Her voice breaks.

It's real emotion.

Real.

And yet, I still don't believe her. Maybe I'm deluding myself because I can't handle the truth. But before we consider giving her back to Andrea, I need to be sure she loves him and not me. If not, then I'm risking her life to save Ri's. And I won't allow that. We'll find a way to save them both. I just don't know if Rialta needs saving yet or not.

"Prove it," I say.

Her eyelashes flutter. *Is she holding back tears?*

"Prove that you don't love me, that you love him."

"How?"

Andrea fucking her floods my memories.

Her moans.

Her legs spread.

Her wanting.

Was it real?

My brain can't remember her reactions. I can't remember if her moans were fake or real. I can barely even remember how he fucked her. Everything about that moment is foggy. *Did it even really happen, or did my mind conjure up that moment in my nightmares?*

That's when the idea hits me. It's risky, but it's the only way I can think to test her.

"By fucking Hayes."

CHAPTER 10

Rialta

WHAT GAME IS *Lennox playing at? What he's asking makes no sense. Does he have a concussion? Has he gone insane? Is he trying to punish me for loving someone else?*

"You're a monster," I growl.

"You already knew that," he grins.

"I don't understand. How will me having sex with Hayes prove anything to you?"

"Trust me, it will prove everything to me." He circles me like a vulture tracking a near-death animal. He's not going to kill me, but I still feel uneasy about this.

"I don't want to fuck Hayes."

Lennox stops in front of me. His eyes are filled with vicious intent. His jaw clenches—he's scared.

He doesn't want to test me any more than I want to fuck Hayes. I don't know how this test is going to prove anything, but I won't back down from a challenge. I'll play his game and figure out how to win if I have to.

"If you do it, I'll send you back to Andrea in exchange for Ri," Lennox says.

"No matter what happens between Hayes and me? No matter what you see? That's the only way I'll consider it."

Lennox grinds his teeth. It's not the agreement he wants. He wants to have a chance at keeping me—but he'll never have that chance again. I'm not his. He can't keep me. I'm deciding my own fate from now on.

"So what will it be? I fuck Hayes, and you send me to Andrea. Otherwise, you can play your little games with someone else."

"If you have sex with Hayes, I'll send you back to Andrea if that's still what you want." His words are a promise—but I'm not sure I trust him. He loves me, and love will make you do crazy things.

I hold out my hand. He sucks in a breath as he takes it in his—like my touch burns his skin. When I feel his hand in mine I feel the same burn. But neither of us lets go as we shake on the deal—both of us hiding plenty from the other.

Finally, we let go at the same time.

Lennox leaves the room; I assume to go talk to Hayes.

I fold my arms over my chest, thinking about the deal I just made and how I feel about it. *Why does Lennox want me to fuck Hayes?* I doubt Hayes will even agree to it. But if he does...

If he does, I'll fuck him. I'm not a prude. It doesn't matter who I love—I like Hayes, and I have no problem enjoying a sexy man. *But what does Lennox think he's going to figure out by watching us have sex? Am I supposed to fight Hayes? Am I supposed to give in? Not enjoy it? Call out Andrea's name?*

I'm not sure how to play this game.

Lennox enters the room again with a hesitant Hayes right behind him. Lennox pushes the dresser back in front of the door. Then we all just silently stare at each other.

It's clear Lennox has told Hayes what he wants him to

do. Usually, Hayes would already be flirting with me, giddy with the excitement to tease me. But he's not acting that way now.

I frown. I'm not going to fuck a man who doesn't want it. Hayes looks broken and wounded and terrified.

"Leave us for a minute, Lennox." I look at Hayes as I speak.

"No," Lennox answers.

"If you want us to do this, you'll give us a few minutes alone."

"No," Lennox says again, giving me a hint into why he wants me to fuck Hayes. He thinks he can read my reaction. If I talk to Hayes, we might plan something that will make it easier for me to hide my emotions.

"Step outside or our deal is off," I bark, looking at Hayes.

Lennox growls, but I hear him scooting the dresser once more, and then he's gone.

"He's listening on the other side of the door," Hayes says.

"I know because he's a dick like that!" I raise my voice.

It makes Hayes chuckle.

I smile and then immediately drop it into a serious look. "Do you want to fuck me?"

Hayes blinks. "I'm not sure how to answer that without getting into trouble."

"Forget about Lennox. Forget about our situation. Forget about whatever happened between you and Lennox. Forget about River. If you and I had just met at a bar and got to talking, would you want to fuck me?"

Hayes chews on his bottom lip, unsure how to answer. He's a good-looking man. I love the combination of messy man bun and thick-framed glasses. I've always wanted to fuck a man with long hair and feel what it feels like to have his thick mane in my hands. And Hayes is the type of man who I know is wild in the bedroom. He's fucked a lot of women and always made sure they had a good time. I know he'd know how to show me a good time. He wouldn't be demanding and controlling like Lennox.

But I'll only do it if he wants to and if he can be himself.

I lift Lennox's shirt off, revealing my body in the tight lace lingerie. I'm quickly regretting still wearing it as it's starting to dig into my skin. That is until he looks at me like he wants to devour me.

I grin. "There's the man I know."

Hayes blushes.

I shake my head. "So you find me attractive, but do you want to fuck me? This will only work if you are yourself. I want to fuck you, Hayes, but not the depressed version of you."

He frowns, still not answering me.

"I know you've shared women with Lennox and Gage before. That's all this is—sharing me."

I lick my bottom lip.

"I want you—I want to fuck you, but you don't want me. And I refuse to rape a woman. Even one who pretends she's okay with it."

"Remove your shirt."

Hayes does.

I let myself enjoy him, his hard muscles, and his single Retribution King tattoo. Then I see his grin and the light in his eyes. He likes me looking at him.

We're both hurting, and we both need some pleasure. Something with no strings attached.

"Let's have fun with this," I whisper, avoiding Lennox's snooping.

Hayes's grin widens, and he nods.

"Come back in, Lennox, before you miss all the fun," I

say. Hayes launches himself at me, scooping me up before Lennox is even back in the room.

Lennox doesn't say anything, but I can hear him scooting the dresser back in front of the door.

My legs wrap around Hayes's thin waist as he palms my ass with a playful twinkle in his eyes. His lips crash onto my bottom lip like a puffer fish sucking me into his mouth.

It startles me, making me laugh.

Hayes laughs as well but doesn't let go.

God, he's fun.

I need fun.

He needs fun.

Fuck Lennox and whatever game he's playing at. I'm not going to try and win. I'm not going to change my reaction so I can win the game. I'm just going to enjoy myself.

Hayes's lips hover over my ear in a burning heat. "That's my girl. I won't do anything to hurt you. Don't think about him. Just let me bring you pleasure."

"Yes," I breathe as his tongue circles the outer rim of my ear. "Fuck yes."

He kisses down my neck, and I close my eyes—forgetting who is kissing me. I don't care that it's not Andrea or Kit or Lennox. I simply enjoy the kisses on such a sensitive area.

My hands slide up his neck and begin to tangle in his hair, pulling his hair free from his bun.

He grins and looks at me with a funny expression.

"What?" I ask.

"What is it about the bun that makes every woman I'm with do that as soon as I let them?"

I bite my lip and laugh. "I don't know. It's fun. You're fun."

"What do you want?" he asks.

"I want to have fun. I want to forget and just enjoy this."

"Any positions? Fantasies that have yet to be fulfilled?"

I shake my head. "Fuck me however you want, Hayes. I'm yours."

Both of our eyes cut for a split second to where Lennox is leaning against the wall in the corner of the room—simultaneously watching us and his phone, monitoring the hallway for safety. He doesn't react to me saying I'm Hayes's. And he doesn't tell us to stop. He's going to let us fuck.

Hmmm.

Hayes turns my chin back to him. "Stop thinking of him. I want you thinking of me."

My eyes drop down his body to his pants.

"I'm bigger," he winks.

I laugh again. *Why couldn't I have fallen for a man who makes me laugh like him?* Instead, I fell for every serious man on the face of the earth.

Then his lips are on mine, shutting up my brain because, damn, does the man know how to kiss.

He guides us back toward the bed and then drops me on my back. He flashes me his signature grin, making me laugh.

I expect him to manhandle me the way Lennox would, but instead, Hayes kneels on the floor between my legs. His hands start massaging my feet as he lands gentle kisses slowly up the inside of my legs.

I glance down at him as he inches higher. His long dark hair is a tangle of mess. His eyes pierce me through his glasses. And his grin—god, it's the most infectious thing. I don't know how he turns the sunshine on so easily when just a moment before he was so gloomy. He's a hot god of sun rays, but he's not mine, and I'm not his.

I trust him, though.

And I need this.

So I close my eyes and hope that Hayes doesn't ask me to look at him when he fucks me.

His lips kiss my inner thigh.

I laugh as he hits a ticklish spot. I relax my legs, spreading them wider for him.

He doesn't say anything, and neither do I.

But his tongue flicks over my slit, and I melt into him. I keep my eyes closed, letting my body feel all the wonderful sensations flooding my body. His tongue laps over my sensitive bud again, and I lose all thought. I forget where I am, who I'm with, and what I'm doing.

His hands travel all over my body—feeling every sensitive piece of flesh. And then he lifts me to a sitting position, sits behind me, and eases me onto his lap.

He sweeps my hair to one side as he kisses my neck, and his other hand travels down the side of my breast and stomach before dipping between my legs.

"You're soaked," he whispers.

"Yes," I moan as his fingers circle my clit, making me even wetter.

I lean against his hard chest. He's a warm, hard body. He's a man I could love, but he's not my man.

"Spread your legs," Hayes whispers with his hot breath against my ear.

I do, and I feel extra heat between my legs. I don't think of why that is—but my subconscious knows why, and I like it. I like *him* watching, no matter how I feel about him.

"Fuck me," I moan loudly.

"You sure?" he asks.

I lick my lips but keep my eyes closed. I can feel the heat of his gaze on me.

"Fuck me," I say again.

There's some fumbling behind me, and then he lifts me up until I'm straddling his legs. He lowers me slowly, and soon I feel the tip of cock at my entrance. He releases his grip on my hips—giving me the final move.

My eyes flick open a sliver, and I see Lennox.

His eyes are intense, but I swear I see his lips curl up. *Does he think I'm going to stop this because I love him or Andrea?* He's fucking wrong. I'm going to fuck Hayes because I want to. Because I deserve to feel good, to have a good no strings attached fuck.

I push down onto Hayes's cock, and my eyes fall shut again, feeling him stretching me.

He wasn't joking when he said he was bigger. He's the biggest I've ever had. His hands lift me at the hips as he gently rocks into me.

"Is that...?"

"I'm pierced," Hayes grins against my ear.

I grin. "Fuck, it feels incredible."

"For me too."

And then we move faster—fucking like we've been starved of affection for years.

I ride him hard and fast, while he keeps my legs spread and my body hot and wet. He knows exactly how to touch me, how to keep me wet, how to bring me to climax.

Before I realize its familiar build, I'm coming all over his cock.

I spread my body wide as I do, falling back against Hayes and screaming as I come, unable to hold back.

Hayes lifts me off of him as the last of my orgasm leaves my body. I glance back at him and realize he's still hard. He didn't come.

I kneel in front of him and take his cock in my hand.

"You don't need to—"

I cut him off as my mouth takes him deep into my throat. I slide up and down his thick shaft as his piercing tickles the back of my throat.

I laugh, and the vibration makes him come down my throat.

When I sit back, we're both laughing.

He wipes some of his cum off my bottom lip and winks at me.

We always shared a strange connection me and him. Apparently, it was chemistry, and he's great in bed.

I turn and face Lennox.

"I'm going back to my guard duty, but I'm always free whenever you want my cock again, princess," Hayes says.

"I'll let you know," I grin back before Hayes sneaks out.

I turn back to Lennox, who is still leaning against the wall in the corner of the room.

I raise my eyebrow at him. "Did you figure out who I love, or do I need to fuck Hayes again?"

He smirks and walks toward me. He brushes his hand through my hair, and I stop. I can barely breathe. He won— whatever game we were playing, he thinks he won.

Fuck.

His grin grows larger. "Haven't you figured it out yet, my wife? I know you. I've read your darkest fantasies. I know how much you wanted to be fucked by a friend while your husband watched."

My eyes widen. I had forgotten that I had written that fantasy down. Forgotten that Lennox has my journal.

"You don't love Andrea. If you did, you wouldn't be able to fuck Hayes so easily."

"I don't love you."

Lennox shrugs. "Maybe, maybe not. But I can make you fall back in love with me as long as you don't love another man. You just proved that by how much you enjoyed fucking Hayes. You spread your legs wide and basically begged me to watch. You're mine."

"You're wrong."

"I'm not."

"You are. Now take me back to Andrea and trade me for River."

Lennox's face falls as he realizes he lost after all. Even if I like him more than Andrea—I'm still choosing Andrea, not him.

Lennox

THERE'S a knock at the door. I open it to find Hayes with a pile of clothes. He hands me the clothes before shutting the door again.

I hand Rialta the pile after taking one of the T-shirts for myself. Rialta silently heads to the bathroom, leaving me to question everything I've witnessed.

She may still want to go back to Andrea, but I'm not sorry for the deal I made with her. I know the truth: she doesn't love him.

But she still hates me. She hates me for killing Kit. That's something I'm not sure I'll ever make up to her, but I'll spend my entire life trying.

I'm a man of my word, but I won't send her back to Andrea. She is right that the best way to get Ri back is to trade. Rialta is who Andrea really wants. We just need to find a way to use her as bait to get Ri back, while not actually turning Rialta over to Andrea.

Watching her with Hayes should have been torture— but watching her get such pleasure was fucking hot. I'm hard as a rock now, and I'll never forget the sounds she made as Hayes was fucking her.

He and I have shared plenty of women before. I trust him with my life and hers. I had forgotten that. Watching them together restored my faith in him. He always knows how to give a woman good, selfless pleasure. He always puts their needs above his own. Every woman that's ever fucked him wants to marry him, but all of them know he can't be tamed. He likes fun—not a lasting relationship.

I knew she wouldn't sleep with me no matter what she feels for me. She wouldn't touch Hayes if she loved Andrea. And if she didn't love Andrea, then she needed something to help her forget being violated by Andrea.

Hayes helped her heal from that trauma.

I got to watch my wife being pleasured.

Hayes and I healed our relationship.

And I got my answers.

But now what?

Rialta opens the bathroom door. Gone is the lingerie, and here are leggings and an oversized blue sweatshirt.

"I'm ready. Take me to Andrea," she says.

I sigh.

"We need to talk to Gage and Beckett to form a plan. I'm not just turning you over to him without assurances that he has Ri."

She nods and brushes past me. I follow her out to where Hayes is standing in the hallway. His eyebrows shoot up as she marches past him without a glance, her feet angrily pounding the ground as she walks.

"You pissed her off already? After all I did to relax her, you've already fucked that up?" Hayes teases me.

"Drop it," I growl.

Hayes chuckles and follows us to the living room.

"Beckett! Gage!" Rialta hollers down the hallway.

They poke their heads out of a room and find us in the living room. Beckett doesn't stop gripping his waist, where I know he keeps his gun.

"I'm going to help you get River back. You don't need to shoot me or torture me," Rialta snaps at Beckett.

He removes his hand from his gun. "How?"

"By trading me to Andrea for her. He wants me. He loves me. He wants to be the Corsi heir and for me to marry him and have his babies."

Beckett looks to me, but I'm stone silent.

It's a lie, but I'm not giving away my own plan—not yet.

"How do we ensure he has Ri and Andrea will return her safe and sound?" Beckett asks.

"You make me your hostage and threaten to impregnate me with one of your babies. Vincent has already agreed to make whoever knocks me up his heir. Andrea loves me—but he loves the idea of taking over my father's job more."

Beckett's face softens. "You don't have to do this."

"But I want to—not just to get River back, but because you're right, Beckett. I'm not on your side. I'm your enemy; if enemies, we have to be. I want to be with Andrea. I choose Andrea," she says.

Beckett stares at me, waiting for me to tell him the truth. He seems to have calmed down from earlier when he was trying to torture information out of her now that she's speaking freely.

Gage is also staring at me, waiting.

But I have no answer to give them. The test I gave her tells me she doesn't love Andrea. But that doesn't mean she hasn't chosen him to be her husband, just that she doesn't love him. But for some reason, she thinks he will make her happy, that he will protect her, that he will be a better heir, a better father, better everything.

Hayes is the only one not looking at me. He's staring her down. "Like hell you choose Andrea."

Everyone's eyes whip to Hayes.

"Just because I fucked you doesn't mean I love you, Hayes," Rialta says.

Gage's eyebrows shoot up in amusement. Beckett glares at Hayes disapprovingly.

Hayes chuckles, shaking his head. "You're not in love with me. But you sure as hell aren't in love with Andrea."

"Why does everyone think they know who I love? Did you all gain mind-reading capabilities in the time I was gone? You don't know me. You've never known me. I'm not your precious Ri! I'm not her. I'm not in love with all of you. I'm not your friend. I have my own agenda. And I want to choose my own life. I was forced into a marriage with Lennox, but I never loved him. And now that he's killed Kit —I never will love him."

All eyes jump to me as I stand frozen, just watching her, looking for any clue as to her real agenda. But she just laid it out for all of us. She doesn't love anyone anymore. But she hates me, and Andrea is the only choice she has to get away from me.

Silence stretches between all of us. There is nothing more to be said. I won't force her to stay, and Beckett will do anything to get his wife and unborn child back. She wants to go—so I have to let her.

But she's lying.

She hates me, yes. But that doesn't mean she won't fall back in love with me.

Hayes looks at me with pleading eyes. I just shrug. There's nothing I can do to stop her.

"How do we arrange the trade?" Beckett asks, anxious to get this over with quickly.

"Give me your phone, and I'll call Andrea," Rialta says.

Beckett hesitates but pulls out his phone. "Arrange for the trade on neutral ground."

She nods and then dials a number.

We all stare at her. None of us breathing.

"It's me, Rialta," she says into the phone before pausing. "I'm safe. The Retribution Kings are willing to make a trade —me for River."

All of us scowl when she calls us Retribution Kings, but none of us correct her.

"Dawn at the docks by 31st street," she says before Beckett snatches the phone out of her hand. "And if River or my baby is hurt—we will keep Rialta and fuck her until we've knocked her up. You'll have no chance of becoming her husband or Vincent's heir," Beckett growls into the phone before hanging up.

He looks at the room. "Let's go."

CHAPTER 12

Rialta

RIVER WILL BE SAFE SOON—THAT'S what I focus on as I sit in the back of the blacked-out SUV with my wrists bound together behind my back. We're parked by the docks, waiting for Andrea.

"Are the ropes really necessary?" Hayes asks.

"Yes," everyone else in the car barks at him, including me.

"You're all crazy. This plan won't work," Hayes mutters under his breath.

"If you're smart, you'll leave this city the second you get River back. Leave before we decide you're still a threat to us, and we decide to kill you," I say.

"We're not afraid of Andrea," Lennox says.

"But you're afraid of me. I know your secrets. I know all of you. And if you cross me again, I will kill you all."

I stare Lennox down.

"You still want to kill me, don't you?" he asks.

"I hate you with everything in my body. Nothing has changed."

"Stop bickering; they're here," Beckett says from the

front seat as he stares at the headlights of another SUV driving toward us.

He and Gage get out of the car, while Lennox and Hayes remain in the backseat on either side of me.

Hayes looks at me. "Hate is an awful lot like love. You can only truly hate those that you love."

I shake my head. "You know nothing of love, Hayes."

"What you think you know is wrong."

"I loved Kit. I loved him. He was the man for me, the only person I could ever love, and Lennox killed him in cold blood. Kit didn't belong in this world. He did nothing wrong. But Lennox couldn't have me fucking him while married to him. So he killed him instead of trying to earn my respect. I'll never forgive him."

Lennox sits silently—he knows I speak the truth and has given up. I hope he has. I hope after I get out of this car I never have to see Lennox again.

"I like you, Hayes. I don't want to hurt you. And I want Ri and her baby safe. Beckett won't take any convincing to leave. Gage won't either. Go with them somewhere safe and far away. If you want your friend here to live—you'll take him with you, too," I say.

Hayes frowns but doesn't say anything. I hope he heeds my warning because the only person who deserves to die is Lennox. The rest of them are innocent enough. If they leave, we'll let them live.

We all squint through the front window as we hear a car door slam. Andrea and one of his men get out of their car, squaring off against Beckett and Gage. There's no sign of River yet.

Lennox grabs onto my arm, even though my arms are tied behind me, and he and Hayes sit on either side of me.

"Is that really necessary?" I glare down at where he's holding onto my arm.

"Yes," he hisses.

"Where is Ri?" I hear Beckett say to Andrea.

"Where is Rialta?" Andrea counters.

I tense. Of course, neither of them is going to yield to the other. They both want proof first.

Beckett glances back at me through the window, trying to figure out how to get Ri back with desperation in his eyes.

"Show me to Andrea. Show him that you brought me. He wants me and trusts me. He'll listen to me when I tell him to hand over River." I'm not sure Beckett can hear me, but Lennox can. He opens the door and pulls me out.

Hayes slides out after me and both men flank me as we walk forward to a foot behind Gage and Beckett.

"She's safe, and we're happy to return her in exchange for my wife," Beckett growls.

"Rialta, are you okay? Did any of them hurt you? Did any of them try to fuck you?" Andrea says.

"I'm—" Gunfire rains down on us, interrupting my reply.

Everyone ducks on instinct, trying to shield themselves from the bullets, but I sense Lennox and Hayes reaching for me. I only have a split second to decide what to do. If I stay and let them protect me, I'll be dragged back into the bullet-proof car and driven away.

I'm tired of being protected.

And I know what I have to do.

I run.

I run straight toward Andrea—who is also ducking down as he slinks back toward his car.

Lennox shouts my name, but his words won't stop me.

Beckett is running a foot ahead of me, not even bothering to duck or swerve to keep the bullets from hitting him. It's clear the only thing on his mind is getting to that car before Andrea jumps in and drives away.

I chase after him—needing to see River safe as much as he does. My fate isn't to live a long and happy life, but I'm determined that after all River has sacrificed for me that she does.

A loud boom from behind me has me stumbling on my feet and my ears ringing. I don't stop, though, even though I want to glance behind me. I want to know if Lennox and Hayes and Gage are still alive or bleeding out on the concrete.

I don't let myself look, though, and I can no longer hear their footsteps behind me.

I feel the whoosh of air all around me as bullets whiz by my body. And I don't have to think long to know who is shooting at us. This is the same man who has wanted me dead since birth.

I lock my eyes on the car, knowing I need to get there as quickly as possible. It's my only salvation.

Andrea pulls himself into the driver's seat.

Fuck.

Will he drive off before I get to him? Or will he wait for me?

Beckett's gun aims toward the car.

"No!" I shout, but instead of killing Andrea, Beckett shoots out both front tires until they are flat and undrivable.

I let out a breath but keep running while I remove the ropes from my wrists.

Almost there...

Andrea jumps out and takes off, running towards the dock.

Beckett beats me to the car and throws open the back door, not bothering to go after Andrea. Two seconds later, I'm opening the other door, but Beckett's unearthly screams tell me what I'm going to find.

No.

My heart clenches in my chest as I look into the backseat.

It's empty.

My shoulders slump.

Thank god. She's not dead—she's just not here. Andrea lied. Or he has her hidden somewhere else.

Damn him.

Beckett takes off after Andrea, and I take off after him. The ring of bullets grows more distant with every step we take. The man who wants me dead isn't chasing us. It makes me wonder if he really wants me dead or just afraid. If he just wants to ruin every important moment of my life. Maybe he wants me to live in fear, scared to leave my house, until the day comes when he decides to kill me.

Another thought unfurls in my mind, but I shut it up quickly. I know it's correct as I rest my hand on my stomach.

"Ri!" Beckett shouts through the harbor, looking for any sign that Andrea stashed her somewhere among the boats.

I run faster.

I come to a fork in the road—Beckett turns left, but something tells me to turn right.

I slow, trying to let my gut lead the way. I hear footsteps rush by, but one set turns in this direction.

Lennox.

I don't have much time, but I don't need much.

I stare at the boat to my right. There's nothing special about it. No sign of anyone on it, but the softest of moans echoes through me.

I take a step toward the boat as Lennox's hand grabs my bicep.

"Rialta," he breathes out in a huff.

"Listen," I say.

"You're bleeding," he says.

I shake my head. I don't care that I'm bleeding. I don't feel anything, so the wound can't be serious.

"Listen," I urge him again.

He glares at me, but I can tell he's listening, and he hears it. His eyebrows draw together. His hand travels down my arm until he's gripping my hand, weaving our fingers together.

It burns, his touch. But I don't pull away, needing to get to the person behind the sound as quickly as possible.

He feels the same way because he doesn't tell me to stay. Together, we jump on the boat and find the dark shadow of a human in a tied-up ball on the top deck. They were laid here for us to find.

"River!" I cry out when I see blood pooled around her.

Lennox and I run to her at the same time, kneeling on either side of her. Lennox eases the hood off, careful not to injure her head or neck, that could already be injured.

And then we both gasp.

It's not River.

The body with a weak breath, moaning just soft enough to let us know he's alive, is Kit.

CHAPTER 13

Lennox

RIALTA and I stare at Kit, who is lying on the bed in a safe house Gage found on the outskirts of the city. We didn't think it was safe to go back to the apartment we were in before. Not with so many people after us, and not when we have no idea what happened to Kit.

Gage left to join Hayes and Beckett to search for Ri the second he helped us get Kit here.

"What do we do?" Rialta asks, staring at him. "Should we call a doctor? Should we have taken him to the ER?"

"No, he's better off here."

She looks at me deeply, as if unsure if she can trust me or not.

"Kit's breathing. His heart rate is fine. His blood loss minimal. Most of his wounds seem to have healed. He's been tortured, but not for a while. We can stitch up the remaining injuries, give him some pain meds, and help him sleep."

"But what if he has internal injuries?" she says, her voice full of worry.

"Then we'll take him to the hospital."

Her head snaps to me.

"I'll take him myself. I promise," I say.

Her eyes don't blink as she bores into mine. And then she nods slightly, accepting my promise.

"Let's get him undressed to see if there are any other injuries we need to address."

"Okay," her voice is breathy. She pulls out the scissors from the first aid kit we always travel with and begins cutting down the middle of his T-shirt. She gently pulls the pieces of cloth off, and we both wince. His torso is covered in dark shades of purple. There's a deep slice across one of his pectoral muscles that could use some stitching.

Rialta's eyes dash to me, waiting for my assessment—trusting me with the man she loves.

"He's okay—I'll stitch up that wound in just a minute. Cut off his pants first, though."

She nods. Her hands shake as she cuts down his pant legs. Tears well in her eyes, and her face turns white as a ghost as she looks at the slices on his legs.

"Kit's going to be okay. He's going to live. And you and him are going to live happily ever after."

Her face turns whiter, and I think she's going to pass out on me.

"Rialta!" I grab her hands and shake her gently. "He's going to live, and so are you. You'll marry him and have babies with him and live your life with him."

Her eyebrows pinch together, and her lips quake. "We won't," she whispers.

"He's going to live. I promise. Why don't you go get him some water and food while I stitch him up? He'll need something to regain his strength when he wakes up."

She squeezes her eyes shut and shakes her head before taking his hand in hers, holding it tightly. "I'm not leaving him. He didn't deserve this. He wasn't supposed to be in this life. This is my fault."

I sigh but don't say anything else. There are no words I can offer that will comfort her now.

I take the supplies out of the first aid kit and go to work stitching him up as much as I can, ignoring his naked body and the way she stares at him with eyes full of love and worry. I would give everything for her to look at me the way she does him.

I do my best work, stitching him quickly and efficiently. She holds his hand the whole time, while the other runs over his forehead and through his hair.

I wipe off the excess blood on his skin and pull the bedsheets over his body. Silence stretches through the room, the air thick with tension as we watch him and wait. Neither of us is willing to leave. She's not willing to leave him. And I'm not willing to leave her.

A moment later, he stirs.

"Rialta?" he croaks.

"Shhh, I'm here. Just rest—you're safe now," she exhales as if trying to convince herself that he's safe.

"Do you remember what happened? Who took you?" I ask.

Kit looks at me, but I can tell his head is still groggy. Finally, he says, "No."

"I'll give you some privacy. Let me know if you need anything." And then I walk out.

After leaving the bedroom, I don't make it far before collapsing onto the living room couch. I should make food to bring them, but I'm spent. And I don't have the emotional energy to witness any more of their shared longing or the kisses I'm sure she's coating him in.

Kit's alive. And I helped to ensure he stays that way.

He's alive—she no longer has a reason to hate me, to want me dead.

He's alive—the love of her life is back in the picture. I have no chance with her.

He's alive...

I smile.

I'm happy for her. At the same time, my heart is breaking.

"Did you mean what you said?" Rialta says from the doorway.

My head whips to her, shocked she left Kit so soon.

"Is Kit okay?" I ask.

"I gave him some pain pills, and he fell back asleep. I figured it was best to let him rest."

I nod.

"Did you mean what you said?"

She doesn't have to explain what she meant. I know.

"If you love Kit, if you choose Kit, I'll help you get him forever."

"What about our deal?"

"Forget about our deal. It doesn't matter. It doesn't matter what Andrea wants, or Vincent wants, or anyone else. The only thing that matters is what's in your heart. If it belongs to Kit, then as soon as he's well enough to travel, I'll get you two somewhere safe."

She wraps her arms around her torso, blood covering her shirt and hands. Sweat greases her hair. She walks over, my eyes never leaving her as she sits on the couch next to me but not touching.

I still, unsure of why she's not holding vigilance over Kit.

"When did you start loving me? Why? What changed?" she asks.

With her sitting here, and her boyfriend in the next

room, this feels like my last chance to make her mine. I won't get another shot. This is it.

"The second I pulled you out of the car when I thought Kit was raping you."

"No, you hated me then."

I nod. "Hating you was only possible because I also loved you."

I watch her carefully. Her chest slows, and her breathing evens. Her ears seem to strain to catch every word out of my mouth.

"You were wild and free and knew what you wanted out of life. You were determined to decide your own fate. And so fucking strong—it took my breath away to see someone that strong, knowing how many people wanted to kill them. It didn't deter you. You were sunshine to my gloom."

"I wasn't strong—I was just surviving the only way I knew how."

My eyes blaze. "You did more than just survive."

She stills, my words sinking in.

"I did it because I had to—"

"No, you did it because you were strong. You made it easy for me to be strong and for all of us. We were only strong because of you."

She fidgets on the couch.

"Do you truly love me, or is it just something nice you're saying so I'll pick you?"

I tilt my head. "You already know the answer to that. Just like I know you loved me back before you spiked my drink and Andrea kidnapped me."

She blinks but doesn't deny nor confirm it.

"Hayes and I once had a conversation about you. He told me you would never love again, that you couldn't love again. You say you love me, but do you really? Do you love me the way you loved before?"

I don't know why she's asking me this. She probably wants me to lay my heart out for her before she crushes it. I have no chance with her, but I love her too much for her not to know the truth—all of it.

"No, I don't love you the way I loved before."

Her face falls as she stares at her hands in her lap. I swear I see a hint of disappointment sweep across her face.

"I love you more," I say.

Her eyes snap up, meeting mine with an emotion I can't read.

"Her name was Iris," I continue.

Rialta holds her breath, willing me to tell her everything. If she has to make a decision about which man she will spend the rest of her life with, she deserves to have all the facts. So I'll tell her everything I can.

"I met her when I was sixteen. She was hanging off of Hayes's arm, and her lipstick was smeared across his cheek. At this point, Hayes and I hadn't shared women. Once one of us claimed someone, she was off limits to everyone else. But when Iris turned and looked at me—I fell. It was love at first sight. I fell for her piercing eyes, her curious smile, and her infectious laugh.

"But so did Hayes. And Gage. And our friend Caius. How could we not? She was an angel. Sweet, innocent, and the kindest soul. Even though she grew up as a Retribution King's child, she hadn't seen the darkness we had. She didn't believe in revenge. She had never gotten her hands bloody. And she had no intention of ever doing so."

I close my eyes, the burning pain rising up in my chest again.

"She was innocent, unlike me," Rialta says.

I shake my head. "She was naive because he had never seen how cruel the world is. You've had to run from darkness your whole life. Iris only saw the good in people. She didn't see me as this evil monster, capable of slaughtering men and then still sleep like a baby at night.

"Iris was the first woman we all competed over; the first woman we all wanted. If we had met her a few years later, we would have shared her like we did other women until she made her choice. But I was a selfish bastard, and I couldn't stand to see her with any of the others. Lucky for me, the second she saw my affection for her—she was mine."

Rialta's tongue flicks across her bottom lip.

I swallow hard before continuing, ignoring the way my body hardens at her smallest gesture.

"Once Iris was mine, I vowed to do everything I could to maintain her innocence. I vowed to protect her from the cruelty of the world, to keep her safe and protected. And once the others saw how much we loved each other, they vowed to protect her with their lives as well. None of the others had serious girlfriends, so Iris had all of our protection."

My heart clenches in my chest, the next part hard to get out.

"I didn't rush our relationship. We had our entire lives for all of our firsts..."

"You mean, you didn't fuck her?" Rialta asks.

"Iris was a virgin. We were young, and I was happy to take my time with her. Taking my time with all of her firsts, but then..."

I squeeze my eyes shut as the pain of it all hits me. How stupid and naive I was. How I and the others failed to protect her.

A calming hand rests on my thigh, and I open my eyes, trying to hide my surprise at Rialta's touch. She'll remove her hand if I show my shock.

With her calming presence, I have the strength to continue. "In the Retribution Kings, you're to be initiated when you turn eighteen. The initiation is different for each person. It's customized to ensure that it tests each individual's strengths and weaknesses."

"And Iris was your weakness," Rialta says.

"She was my weakness and my strength. I would have never endured the trials without her, but then..." my voice catches. It's hard to share one of the worst moments of my life.

Then again, I've had many worse moments with Rialta since then.

"The initiation was hard. They made me hurt my friends in ways I wasn't sure we'd ever recover from. They played tricks on my mind in addition to burdening my physical body. I thought I had finished, I thought it was over, and then...and then I saw Iris." Tears burn my eyes as I relive my failure. "Iris, my sweet, innocent girlfriend was tied to a bed being fucked by a dozen men." I shake my head as the tears fall.

"I should have fucked her the night I told her I loved her, and she said the words back. I should have been her first. She begged me to be her first, but I was stupid—I wanted to keep her pure from my darkness as long as possible. I denied her what should have been hers. I thought I was protecting her, but I gave her to them on a silver platter to destroy."

Her hand squeezes harder on my thigh, giving me the strength to continue.

"I couldn't save her—but I could take my vengeance on them. I killed them. Every. Single. One. I had never killed so many men in a single night."

My eyes are darkness as I speak. Rialta should be terrified of the man she sees in my eyes, but she doesn't move. She's not afraid of me. She's not Iris.

"I was killing them, getting my vengeance, thinking I was protecting her in the only way I knew how—but the last man, he knew what was coming, and he—he took her from me and strangled her before I could get to them.”

My body burns with the pain of what I endured—of what Iris endured. “I don’t deserve to love. I failed the person I vowed to protect. After that, I vowed to never love again. I vowed to spend my life killing anyone who had a hand in her death.”

I look at Rialta. “But then Beckett needed me to take his place so he could be with Ri. So I did it. I knew I’d never love again, unlike Hayes or Gage. I knew I was the only one who could marry you and keep myself from falling for you.”

I swallow the lump in my throat. “I shouldn’t have fallen in love with you. When I first met you, I thought you were Iris made over, but worse. That you were somehow more naive and sheltered from the reality of this world.” I meet Rialta’s gaze. “It didn’t take me long to realize you were my equal. You had experienced the cruelty just like I had, but unlike me, you didn’t bow to it. You didn’t let it level you. You were still living. Still falling in love. Still feeling the sunshine on your face and the rain on your hair. You felt it all, and you weren’t afraid of death. You knew it would probably take you sooner than most, but you weren’t scared of it. And you weren’t afraid of me.”

I put my hand on top of hers, surprised she doesn’t immediately pull it away.

“I’m a cold, cynical man who knows I’m risking every-thing by loving you. We’re both more likely to die before we grow old together. I did everything I could to hate you rather than love you because you have enough enemies. You don’t deserve to add mine to the list. But I couldn’t help it. It’s selfish, me loving you. And it’s why I don’t think you should choose me, no matter how much I want you to. Any other man would be a better choice, Andrea even, and Kit definitely. But it won't stop me from spending the rest of my life hoping you'll be foolish and choose me."

We stare at each other breathlessly, the air all sucked from the room. Our hearts struggle to pump blood through our bodies as we both wrestle with our own feelings.

She loves me—I know she does. But she also loves Kit. And she has some feelings I don't understand toward Andrea. I don't know who she loves the most, though. I'm not even sure she knows. But right now, I just want what's best for her.

"You get to decide your future, Rialta. You get to decide whether you want to be with me, or Andrea, or Kit. And whatever you choose, I'll help you get it. If you choose me, I'll do everything I can to keep from failing you. But I know you don't want my protection. If you were to choose me, it'd be because you'd want an equal. I'll teach you everything I can so you can protect yourself.

"If you choose Andrea, it will be because you want to be protected. He's the safe choice. The Corsi men will follow him without question.

"And if you choose Kit, it's because you choose love above all else. He's your first love, your true love. You'd choose to escape this life and run from it for as long as you can. If you choose him, I'll do everything I can to help you live that life.

"None of these choices are easy or promise you a long future. But I do promise that no matter what you choose, I'll continue to hunt the man down who keeps playing with us until he finally decides it's time for you to die."

I take a breath, swallowing my pride.

"I'm not sure if you've made your choice, but I'll accept whatever you choose," I promise.

She opens her mouth, maybe to tell me her answer, but suddenly she runs.

I frown, my eyebrows pinching in confusion as I chase her. *Why the hell is she running?*

She dashes into a bathroom, not bothering to close the door, as she collapses over the toilet and empties her stomach.

My heart flutters in my chest, already guessing the reason for her sickness. I have no idea what to think other than I'm terrified. Terrified to learn the truth. Terrified for what it means for her. Terrified that it might mean her choices are being taken away once again—something I'll fight with my life to prevent from happening.

She collapses, her hands hanging over the edge of the toilet seat while her head rests on the edge.

I kneel down next to her and tuck her hair back, gently pulling her into my lap. She doesn't resist—she's too exhausted.

I take the moment to enjoy her in my arms, knowing this will be the last time. She won't choose me, but a tiny flutter in my heart hopes she doesn't have a choice once she tells me the truth. I hope her baby is mine, and I'll selfishly get to keep her—even if it's not what she wants.

Slowly, she looks up at me, her eyes watering and her face pale. Her lips tremble as if she's afraid to speak the words out loud.

I wrap my arms around her tighter, trying to comfort her. "It's okay—I know. You don't have to say it. It will be okay."

Her eyes flit back and forth, taking in my words. She takes a deep breath as if my words did comfort her and gave her the strength to speak.

"I'm pregnant."

CHAPTER 14

Rialta

IT FEELS good to tell Lennox, to speak the truth out loud. It finally feels like I can admit the truth to myself. It's at least one less thing I have to keep hidden. As much as I don't want to admit it, it feels good to be wrapped in Lennox's arms.

I'm so tired—all I want to do is sleep. My stomach feels so uneasy—I could puke again at any second. My breasts are heavy, my hormones crazy.

I'm pregnant.

"I'm pregnant," I whisper again, needing to hear myself say it again.

Lennox strokes my hair as his other hand splays over my lower stomach. It's a possessive touch—one that says he wants to claim the baby as his. He doesn't care whose it biologically is. I have no doubt about that.

But I'm also sure Kit would feel the same way, as would Andrea. They all want me. They all want the baby. And Andrea and Lennox want to become the next Corsi leader.

Lennox doesn't ask me whose baby it is. He simply sits with me, letting it sink in. I rest my head back against his chest and can feel his heart thumping wildly, despite how calm he appears.

"I'm sorry," I whisper, closing my eyes. My own heart catches up to his, thrumming in my chest.

"You have nothing to be sorry for."

I shake my head and start to sit up, but Lennox pulls me back against him, and I don't fight him. It's easier to talk to him while seated between his thighs and leaning against his hard chest than looking into his eyes anyway.

"I'm sorry I assumed you killed Kit. I'm sorry I let Andrea take you. I let him torture you. I tortured you. I wanted to kill you. I'm sorry for all the scars on your body that will leave permanent marks. I'm sorry for any trauma or nightmares I've caused you. I'm sorry—"

"Shhh, I know." Lennox tilts my chin up to meet his gaze. "Don't apologize. You thought I killed the love of your life. I thought I did too. I deserved it all. Plus, it was worth it if it meant I got to be close to you."

I shake my head, tears burning in them.

"Baby, it's okay. It's okay. I forgive you if that's what you need to hear, but you have nothing to apologize for. I'm just glad he's not dead."

"You mean that?" Looking up at him, my eyes meet his as he nods.

"Yes, I never wanted to take Kit away from you. You were the one to make the decision to kick him out of your life, not me. If he's the man you love, then I'm happy for you, truly."

He means it. He means every word.

"The question is, who kidnapped him? Andrea or The Abyss?"

"The Abyss? Is that what you call the man who's after me, who wants to kill me?" My heart thumps harder in my chest to have any clue as to who he is.

"Yes. He left a business card at the docks with that on it."

"Do we know anything else about him?"

"No, but Gage will have found everything there is to find about him soon enough. Especially if he's the one who took Ri."

I nod.

"Andrea lied to you, Rialta. He either took Kit and framed me to get you to like him, or he knew that someone else took Kit and used that information to turn you against me."

I don't respond. The situation is so much more complex than Lennox realizes, but now isn't the time to explain.

Suddenly, a shadow is cast over us, and we both look up.

"Kit! Are you okay? What are you doing out of bed?" I jump up and go to Kit, who is standing in the doorway, looking much stronger now. The blood seems to have returned to his cheeks, and he isn't moaning in agony.

"I wanted to make sure you're okay," Kit says, staring at Lennox with contempt.

I ignore his look.

"I'm fine. Seeing all your injuries made me sick to my stomach, but I'm better now. I promise." I lean up on my tiptoes as I kiss him.

Kit doesn't hesitate. He kisses me back hard, sweeping his tongue into my mouth and forcing my lips to part. I try to settle into the kiss, to let myself live in the present and enjoy it, but I can't. It's impossible to enjoy the kiss while feeling the heat of Lennox's eyes on the back of my head. I know he's studying my every move and trying to figure me out. That's what his stupid test about Hayes was earlier. But that was when Kit was dead. Now that he's alive—his test was moot.

Kit releases me and stumbles back.

I grab the neck of his shirt, holding him steady.

"We should get you back to bed," I say.

"Only if you come with me." His eyes blaze with need, completely ignoring Lennox and forgetting about the fact that we broke up, and I moved on.

Maybe his torture caused brain damage or amnesia, but our relationship isn't something we need to talk about right now. He needs to rest and, ideally, see a doctor for a full medical assessment, but that will have to wait.

I nod, slinging Kit's arm around my shoulder and beginning to lead him back to the bedroom. He's leaning on me a lot as I take careful steps, carrying more of his weight than I was expecting.

"Here, lean on me too," Lennox says, throwing Kit's other arm around his shoulder.

I mouth 'thank you' to Lennox, and he just nods back.

After several careful steps and Lennox taking most of Kit's weight, we finally get him into bed.

This time instead of leaving, I climb into the bed with Kit—worry marking my face as Kit almost immediately drifts off to sleep. Lennox made himself scarce the second Kit was back in bed, so I'm left to my own thoughts as I lay on my side, watching Kit breathe slowly in and out.

I stroke his cheek.

"I'm so sorry. If you'd never met me this wouldn't have happened." Tears drip down my cheek and onto his pillow. "I tried to protect you. I tried to get you out of my life so you'd be safe. I failed. I'm so sorry." My voice catches as I speak.

"It's not your fault," a deep voice startles me from the doorway.

Lennox.

I quickly wipe my tears as he carries a tray into the room.

"Ginger ale and crackers."

"Thank you," I say.

He sets the tray down on the nightstand next to the bed.

"Do you need anything else? Anything else to eat or drink?"

I shake my head. "No, this is perfect. Thank you."

He nods and stares at Kit. "It's not your fault. It's mine and Andrea's and your father's and The Abyss's, but not yours. Falling in love isn't wrong. No matter who you fall in love with, you can't help it. And he won't fault you for putting him in danger, either. He'd risk his life all over again if it meant getting to love you."

My lips thin at his words, but I don't say anything. Instead, I lean over and pick up a cracker from the tray to munch on, trying to keep my stomach from heaving again.

Lennox's heated gaze never leaves me.

"It's his?" he asks, hope and pain in his eyes.

I look to Kit, making sure he's asleep before I answer.

"Yes."

Lennox exhales a sharp breath before he speaks again. "So you choose him?"

"No." My eyes flit to Lennox, whose face is pulled into a confused expression.

"Then who?"

I can see hope flooding his expressions. I decide to quickly put him out of his misery.

"I choose Andrea."

CHAPTER 15

Lennox

RIALTA IS pregnant with Kit's baby.

But she doesn't want to be with him—she wants to be with Andrea.

And me? I'm pretty sure she still wants me dead, although I don't understand why.

I hold her gaze, completely confused by this woman. I don't know what to believe anymore. I don't know who she is, what game she's playing, or whose side she's on.

I don't know who she loves. *It feels like she's playing all three of us, but why? For what purpose?*

I tilt my head toward the door, hoping to have this conversation in private. She frowns and snuggles into Kit harder, refusing to leave his side.

I roll my eyes. "Follow me, or I'll make sure Kit is awake while you tell me you don't want him to raise his own child."

She glares. "You wouldn't."

I growl, and Kit twitches at the sound, beginning to stir.

She strokes his cheek until he's gently snoring again and

then eases off the bed, following me back into the living room.

"Happy? I promised him I'd stay, but I leave after five minutes."

"Kit will live. You have some explaining to do." I stare at her. I study her belly for any sign of swelling, but I see nothing. My eyes drag up her body to her breasts, but they, too, don't seem any bigger. There is no outward sign of her pregnancy except for the morning sickness.

I think back to Ri's pregnancy and realize it took several months for her belly to begin to show. Rialta can't be very far along.

I cross my arms, my eyes darkening. "Explain yourself."

"There is nothing to explain. I'm free to make any decision I want."

My eyebrows shoot up. "I will support your decisions, but you're still my wife. If I'm going to give you up, then you need to explain to me why. You need to explain everything to me."

"I owe you nothing."

I huff, grabbing her wrist and yanking her to me until her body is flush against mine—face to face.

"You owe me everything, my wife. You have no reason to hate me anymore. I didn't kill your baby daddy. And I'll let you choose who you spend the rest of your life with—whether it be me, Kit, Andrea, or some other bastard. But you owe me an explanation. What's going through that pretty little head of yours?"

"Why?" She grinds her teeth together as she spits back at me.

"Why? Maybe because I've saved you numerous times. Maybe because I'm your husband. Maybe because I married you to save our mutual friends. Maybe because I fucking love you, that's why!"

Her upper lip raises in a snarl as I grip her biceps holding her to me. "Fine. You want to know the truth? The truth is I want Kit safe. I love him. And the only way he has a chance at being safe is if I stay away from him."

I take a deep breath, prepared for all the sassy snark she's about to throw my way. Her justifications will flow now, and I'm ready to dispute every single one of them.

"I want this baby safe, and Kit would want the same. The only person who can keep this baby safe is Andrea."

My chest hollows like she just stabbed me in the heart. Her jaw clenches—she knows that comment stung deep.

"So let me get this straight. You love Kit? You think Andrea can protect you? And you hate me?"

"Seems to sum everything up."

"You still hate me? Even though I didn't kill Kit?"

"Yes."

I lower my head, my lips dropping lower and lower toward hers. I watch her carefully—studying her every reaction and trying to find the truth she refuses to speak out loud.

She tries to remain frozen, unfazed. She tries to keep her impenetrable shield up. But her tongue slips between her lips, unconsciously wetting them as I lower mine toward her.

"Liar," I breathe hot fiery breath onto her lips.

Her eyes narrow in on my lips, revealing more of her true feelings.

"You may love Kit. You may choose Andrea as your protector. But you want me."

She swallows hard, trying to push down her feelings.

I lick my lips, mimicking her movements from before, and her eyes light up at the realization of what she gave away.

She frowns, biting down on her bottom lip. "I'm a woman, and I'm attracted to a lot of men. I fucked Hayes, for goodness sake! It doesn't mean I want him."

"No, you don't want him. You want me."

She tries to pull away, to deny her true feelings, but I grab her wrists in one hand and pull them up in front of us.

"Let me go," she pants.

"No, not until you admit the truth. Not until you tell me what you're up to."

"It doesn't matter if I want you or not. Lust has no place in my decisions. Maybe I'll fuck you one more time before I go back to Andrea, but even if you give me the best damn orgasm of my life, it won't change anything."

"Won't it?" I flash a sexy grin.

She rolls her eyes at me, and they narrow into vicious slits. "No, it won't. Because you still can't protect me and this baby."

"I ca—"

"You can't. You've failed to protect me so far. You couldn't kill the man who's been hunting me all this time. You only just discovered his name—The Abyss."

"No one else has been able to find him either."

"Andrea figured his name out within a week and told me a few days ago. It took you months," she confesses.

I open my mouth again, but she slays me with her words first. "And I'll never love you. I never did, and I never will. I could never love a man that kills so mercilessly. A man so grumpy and sour. A man who can't see the beauty in the world and is still hung up on a dead woman. A man—"

I shut her up by slamming my lips down on her. Her open, mid-sentence mouth lets my tongue easily slip inside and find hers. I kiss her with all I have and wait.

One.

Two.

Three.

Four.

Four seconds—that's how long she allows our tongues to tangle together before she pushes me away.

I release her from my hold.

I let her realize how badly she wants me despite having two other men she wants for different reasons. She could pick any other man on the planet, and they'd be kneeling at her feet, worshipping her every move.

And yet, she wants me.

"Fuck you, Lennox. I hate you!"

"Tell that to your body." My gaze burns up and down her, seeing all the proof I need that she wants me. She hates me, but I still have a chance to change that. As much as I used to think differently, I'm the best man for her.

I can protect her and her baby better than Andrea can. And I can love her more than Kit can. She just doesn't see it yet. I spent all of our relationship hating her and thinking I would never fall in love with her—how foolish I was.

She hammers her fists against my chest as if angry that I caught her in a lie. She's mad that I figured her out. She's confused as hell and can't make any choice. She loves us all and hates us all for different reasons.

But she's most frustrated with me. She wants to love me but doesn't know how. She wants to trust me with her and her baby's life but doesn't know how.

I let her pound her fists into my chest. I let her get out some of that frustration before I crash my lips down on hers again.

This time she's ready for me. Her teeth sink down into my bottom lip until my blood spills into both of our mouths. Instead of letting go, I grab her thighs and pull her up, until she's forced to wrap her legs around my waist.

Our lips are still smashed together, both of our eyes open and locked on each other.

Finally, she pulls her lips free. "I hate you." She spits my blood in my face.

It doesn't phase me. I love how she fights it. I love how she fights me, how she shows me her strength.

"I know, baby, I know. You hate me."

I lean down, and she slaps me across the cheek. I back her against the wall, boxing her in with my body. I need to push her to the limits, so she'll realize her decision is madness. Andrea is the last person she should choose. Anyone else would be better. In the end, she'll realize I'm her match in every way.

Her neck cranes up, and our lips hover again. I'm not touching her, but her lips rise as if she wants to kiss me again but won't allow herself to.

So I close the gap, but this time, I don't crash down on her. Our lips brush together, sending tingles through our bodies, igniting spark after spark all the way to our toes.

"Why do you even want me if you know I hate you?" she whispers, her voice needy and breathy.

My gaze cuts through hers. "You can only hate me this much because you love me."

She lifts herself up until her lips smash into mine, just as the front door opens.

I moan as she jumps off of me before anyone can see us kissing. But anyone with half a brain can tell what was happening.

"Call a doctor," Beckett barks at me as he carries a bloodied and unconscious Ri in his arm. He carries her down the hallway to the first available bedroom with Gage fast on his heels.

"I've already called a doctor, Beckett. She'll be here soon," Gage says.

Rialta and I run down the hallway after them, trying to figure out what we can do to help. But when we get to the open doorway, Rialta slams to stop, causing me to slam into her.

My shoulders slump when I see Beckett and Gage hovering over Ri. Blood soaks her pants. Her belly looks smaller than the last time I saw her. Beckett's face is pure terror as he grips his wife's hand in a prayer, while Gage slowly begins to undress her.

Rialta's hand finds mine, and she squeezes hard as I see a tear roll down her cheek.

Beckett looks up at me in an absolute rage. "Get Rialta out of my sight."

CHAPTER 16

Lennox

I SEE RIALTA'S TEARS. I see her anguish, but it flickers away as quickly as it came until her face is once again a sheet of stone.

I narrow my eyes, trying to figure out once again what game Rialta is playing.

Beckett's voice shatters through my thoughts.

His voice is unlike anything I've ever heard out of him. It's high-pitched, fast, and breathy. I'm sure if you took his blood pressure right now it would be so high that you'd worry about him having a stroke.

Gage is trying to remain strong and in control as he pulls off her blood-soaked pants, and a first aid kit on the bed next to him. But his hands are trembling. He's not easily rattled, but seeing Ri on the brink of death has him shattered.

Hayes rushes in next and, at the sight of her, collapses onto his knees.

"Stay with me, baby, stay with me. You're strong. You have to live. I can't live without you..." Beckett's words continue on and on and on as he grips the love of his life's hand. He won't survive if anything happens to Ri or the unborn baby. I'm not sure any of us will.

The scene is chaotic. No one knows what to do. I don't know how they found Ri or who had her. I don't know Rialta's role in Ri's kidnapping or torture. But I do know that her presence isn't going to help.

I grip her bicep and lead her out of the room. She stumbles after me, her eyes locked on Ri. She's in shock, I realize. We all are.

I pull her after me, knowing I just need to take control of the situation. I push her inside Kit's room.

"If you leave this room, I'll tie you up and torture you until I get every bit of honesty out of you. Even the truth you're desperate to keep hidden." I let my eyes drag to her stomach, so she understands. And then I shut the door, locking it behind me from the outside.

Once I'm back in Ri's room, I take control. "Hayes, go downstairs and wait for the doctor. Get her up here as fast as possible."

I pull him up by the back of his shirt and shake him until I'm sure he's stable on his feet. He shakes his head and then runs out of the room.

Beckett is still mumbling as his hand explores Ri's body, fumbling over her limbs and wiping away blood. Gage has frozen at the sheer volume of blood but no clear injury on which to apply pressure.

Everyone suspects what's wrong, but no one is willing to say the words out loud. And if the worst has happened...I purse my lips, forcing oxygen into my body.

It hasn't.

Ri's alive. Her unborn baby is alive. We got to her in time. And Rialta had nothing to do with this.

I grab gauze from the first aid kit and begin soaking up blood so we can get a better picture of Ri's injuries. I try to think logically and keep my emotions reigned in. It's something I've done countless times when any of us have been injured.

But this is Ri and...*fuck.*

I can barely keep it together. There's so much blood. I check Ri's pulse and find it, but it's weak. Her chest barely rises when she breathes. Her wrists are red with welts and cuts. But mostly, her body is bruised and covered in blood with no outward cut or injury, which worries me more than if there was a cut, a bullet, anything I could remove or stitch up. But this...there is nothing we can do until the doctor arrives.

Where is the damn doctor?

My eyes cut to the door, impatiently waiting for her to get here. At the same time, I'm terrified she's not going to be able to do anything to help Ri.

Please don't let it be too late.

"In here," I hear Hayes say, and my breath catches.

I push Gage back and make room as Hayes leads the doctor to Ri. The doctor is young—maybe thirty. But she doesn't question the scene in front of her.

Each of us holds our breath as the doctor checks Ri's vitals and makes a quick assessment. She doesn't relay what she's found. Instead, she starts IV fluids in her arm. Then her eyes flick to her bag Hayes brought in, and then she looks to me.

"You—stand next to me and pull out equipment as I need it," she orders.

I grab the bag from Hayes and kneel beside the bed. I pull out medications, sutures, oxygen—everything the doctor asks for until finally, the doctor's shoulders relax, and Ri's breathing becomes steady. I grab Ri's wrist and feel a stronger pulse, then look to Beckett and give him a reassuring look.

Tears well in his eyes, and his face has some color in it for the first time since he carried Ri into this room.

"How far along was she?" the doctor quietly asks.

I look to Beckett.

"Umm..." he runs his hand through his hair. "Nineteen, no twenty weeks."

She nods carefully, expressionless. She looks to me as if wanting me to deliver all the news somehow.

"Is...?" Beckett starts but never finishes his sentence.

"Your wife is going to make it. I gave her plenty of fluids and antibiotics to fight any infection that might set in. And..." the woman looks at me, and I know. I know what she knows. I saw her elbow deep inside Ri. And I heard her ask how far along she *was*, not *is*.

Because she's no longer...

The doctor is a smart woman, though. She can tell we are dangerous men. She knows how heartbreaking this is for anyone, let alone under these circumstances, and she knows I'm the one who should say the words.

"Do you have a way to perform an ultrasound, or do we need to take her to the hospital?" I ask, knowing that proof is what Beckett is going to need to face reality.

Her eyes go to her bag. I open the black leather sides wider and find a small device.

"If the baby still has a heartbeat, we'll be able to hear it with this," the woman says.

Everyone stares at the doppler like it's a torture device. That's what it is to us—torture.

The doctor squirts some gel onto Ri's stomach and then moves the device in small movements around her lower belly. Her stomach is already so deflated and deeply bruised we'll need a miracle to hear anything.

The room is absolutely silent.

Beckett closes his eyes like it will help him to hear the heartbeat.

Hayes and Gage hold onto each other in the corner.

I stare at the little machine and then the doctor's features—waiting for the moment of truth.

Quietly, the doctor shakes her head and removes the device from Ri's stomach. She then silently walks outside the room, leaving us to mourn.

I barely make it to Beckett before he collapses in tears.

"This is all my fault! I couldn't protect her! This is all my fault! I couldn't keep our baby safe! I should have never gotten her pregnant! This is all my fault!" he wails over and over.

CHAPTER 17

Rialta

BECKETT'S WAIL cuts deep into my heart. My body quakes with emotion as my hand goes over my own stomach, where my own baby resides. And I know deep down what happened. That they lost their unborn baby.

It's not fair.

It's not fair that Ri and Beckett's baby is gone. A baby that was so wanted. They sacrificed everything to have a child, and it was taken from them, while my unplanned baby is still safe in my belly.

I was never meant to be a mother, but River was. She was born in the role, born to protect innocent life.

While I can't even protect myself, let alone this unborn baby. I can't keep the man I love safe. I can't enact my plan. I'm a failure, and yet my baby is still alive.

It's not fucking fair.

I close my eyes as I listen to Beckett. His voice would break even the cruelest of hearts. It burns through my body and etches itself in my soul. I'll never forget his sounds as long as I live.

It's loud enough that Kit stirs beside me.

"Rialta? Are you okay? What's going on?" Kit asks.

I don't answer him. "How are you feeling?"

"Better. Sore and like I could sleep for a week straight, but better."

"Are you hungry?"

"Only for you," he teases.

I should get him something to eat, but Lennox's words ring in my ear. They believe I'm at fault for Ri losing her unborn baby. And they're right—I am.

It's something I'll have to live the rest of my life carrying with me. Ri is their world. They all love her. Even if she belongs to Beckett, she also belongs to them, too. She saved them. Loved them all. Protected them all. And the hurt she's experiencing is something they won't forgive. They'll want revenge. And no matter how big or small of a role I played in her loss, I'll need to face that punishment.

I consider leaving the room, so Lennox will punish me sooner rather than later, but I decide against it. I sit on the edge of Kit's bed and stroke his hair.

"Kiss me." He licks his lips in anticipation. But I can't think about anything other than Ri.

"I can't," I croak out.

Kit narrows his eyes.

"Good decision." Lennox appears in the doorway as if instantly. There was no sign he was there a second ago, and then all of a sudden, he's here.

I stare at him. Blood covers his body—River's blood.

"Come with me." He barks out, knowing I'll do as he says.

"Rialta, what's happened?" Kit asks.

I ignore him and rise.

"Rialta!" Kit shouts and begins climbing out of bed.

I walk past Lennox before he blocks the door, keeping Kit from exiting.

"Get back in bed before I put you there." Lennox growls.

"Rialta!" Kit shouts again.

"I'm fine. I'll make sure you get some food. Rest—I'll come for you soon and explain everything," I say from behind Lennox.

Kit shakes his head, but Lennox shuts the door on him. A moment later, Gage is standing guard outside the door. He looks over at me like I deserve to die for my sins. Maybe I do.

No, I definitely do.

I glance to the door where I know River is. I want to see her.

"She's alive. And she'll live but without a huge piece of her heart. She will struggle for a long time. So will Beckett," Lennox says.

I squeeze my eyes shut, keeping the pain in. I won't show any emotion. I can't. I don't get to.

"The doctor says she'll need surgery to make sure her womb is clear, but she'll live."

I nod, emotionless.

Lennox looks at me with unveiled disgust. I'm a monster he's just now realizing he's been sleeping with. He dodged a bullet knowing I'm not carrying his baby. Even though we're married, soon he can get rid of me after he punishes me for my role in River's loss.

"Come with me," Lennox says, turning down the hallway away from River.

My hands instinctually rub over my belly as I follow, trying to connect with the tiny being inside me that makes me nauseous and has forced my hand when it comes to what decisions I have to make.

But I don't feel anything, no real connection. Maybe because I never wanted to be a mother. Maybe because the baby isn't big enough to feel yet. I don't feel kicks or movement yet. I haven't even taken a test yet. I haven't gotten an ultrasound. Maybe it's normal for it to not feel real yet. Or maybe I haven't connected with it yet because I don't think this baby has a chance of survival. We'll both be dead before it has a chance of taking its first breath.

Lennox walks through a door, leading me to a set of stairs. He motions for me to go downstairs into pitch blackness.

I don't fight him.

I walk down the stairs, hoping the small piece of love he has for me is enough to let me come back out of this dark basement some day.

I keep my head high, ready to face reality. The love Lennox has for me is fleeting—or most likely long gone, if it ever really existed.

I reach the bottom step and listen to Lennox take each creaky step down the stairs, in sync with my own heartbeat.

The sound stops, and I feel Lennox standing in the darkness with me.

"I can see the truth now," Lennox says.

"What did you figure out?"

"You're the villain. You only care about yourself. I saw it the first time we met, but you made me fall in love with you. You made me think I read you wrong. But now I realize the truth—you're an absolute narcissist. You don't even love the sister who has protected you all these years."

I don't respond. He needs to speak his thoughts. But he waits for me to say anything.

"What's my punishment? Are you going to kill me? Rape me? Torture me? What monster are you going to become to punish me?"

I feel him move toward me until he's an inch away, breathing the same air but not touching me.

"The same monster you are."

I inch closer to him, needing to rattle him, and know that my presence still does that. The problem is his closeness affects me in the same way.

"Does that mean you don't love me anymore? You're back to hating me?" I ask.

I reach my hand out and find his chest inches from me. I drag my hand down his chest, feeling the speed of his heart and the way his breath pulls harder under my touch.

His hand finds my collarbone before creeping up higher and encompassing my neck. His hand squeezes tighter, threatening to cut off my oxygen supply. He's trying to spark fear into my soul, to make me yield to him, to beg for my life—but there will be no begging.

"I never stopped hating you," he growls deeply. It's the kind of growl that reverberates deep into my belly.

"Good," I say, my voice breaking.

He chuckles—half crazy and half angry. I should fear that noise.

"Page nine," he whispers against the shell of my ear.

I gulp, knowing he's referencing my naughty journal. But I'm not going to fuck him. And he doesn't want to fuck me either—he just wants to torture me, bring me to the edge of release before slaughtering me.

He already knows the truth. He's figured it out, finally. He knows what kind of snake I am. This isn't about pulling information out of me—this is about revenge.

"No," I whisper back so softly I'm not sure he heard me.

His hand tightens around my neck as he walks me back until I'm pressed against a brick wall.

I can't see him in the blackness, and he can't see me. But I've never felt like our hearts were in the open, bleeding for each other more than I do now. We're both suffering alone in this dark basement.

"Why?" he breathes.

"Why not?" I purr back, taunting him.

"You think this is all a game? You risked Ri's life. And you killed…"

"I killed her unborn baby. Don't worry, she can get pregnant again. But it seems selfish of her to have tried to have a baby while she's still in this dangerous crime family."

His growl shuts me up, but my words have the intended effect on him. He shoves me harder against the brick wall. "Are you trying to get me to snap your neck?"

"You're going to anyway. I'm just trying to get this over with so I don't have to spend hours being tortured."

His hand loosens on my neck instead of tightening. I pushed too far.

His other hand runs down my body—over every bony curve until his hand rests on the swell of my stomach. And I know what he's not saying—he won't hurt me as long as I'm pregnant. He won't take an innocent life.

"Really? I would think you'd want me to miscarry. You don't have a chance at claiming me or my father's throne while I'm pregnant with another man's baby."

He chuckles. "First, I don't believe a word you're saying right now. I have no idea whose baby is inside you. And second, even if the baby isn't mine, I always find a way to get what I want."

"So do I."

"What do you want, wifey? What is your endgame?"

I tilt my head up. "I thought you'd figured that out. Maybe you're not as smart as I thought you were."

"Well, I'm about to figure it out." His hand tightens quickly, cutting off my breath.

I don't struggle. I remain as still as a statue. I'm not afraid of him any more than he is of me. But my head begins to spin and I begin to see spots. I'm on the edge of passing out when he releases me.

I gasp, sucking in gulps of air and bending over in pain.

"Hmmm, I don't think you're ready for page nine. How about page three?" he says.

Page three? Shit, I don't remember what I wrote. But I do know my heart won't survive it if he fulfills any of my fantasies.

Suddenly, he lifts my shoulders and slams me back against the wall, one of his hands forcing my wrists above my head. His other hand palms my stomach, rubbing carefully over where my bump will be, before slipping between the waistband of my pants.

I can't conceal my shock as his fingers push between my folds, aggressively claiming my body. It's the worst kind of torture, because he owns my body. He knows every inch of it. He knows how to pleasure me and make me scream his name. I'd walk to my own death to feel this pleasure again and again, and he knows it.

No matter which man I choose, Lennox will be the only man who can do this to my body. He's the only one that can touch me and instantly make me his—to control, to claim.

I moan as his fingers rub over my sensitive clit, and I writhe against the wall. I am trying to think about what I fucking wrote on page three to prepare myself, but my mind is so flooded with endorphins and blissfully enjoying his touch. It's impossible to think clearly.

His lips press against my jaw, pushing my brain further away from thoughts and toward that place only he can take me.

I love sex. I love being fucked by a man. It makes me feel

powerful knowing how they worship my body, how I can control them with the touch of their cock. But right now, I've never felt more powerless.

My thighs tighten, squeezing his fingers unconsciously.

Fuck, I'm going to come in a matter of seconds. But right before I find relief, he stops. My body is thrumming with fast-pumping blood and unbridled surges of deep desire with no release.

I search for his eyes in the dark to see the wicked gleam I know is there. Instead, I hear a soft chuckle against my ear. Suddenly, I remember the insane fantasy I wrote on page three. That writing was a huge mistake.

"No," I breathe.

"No? No, you don't want me to touch you again?" I can hear the cruel smile in his voice.

I don't answer. I can't win. He's going to torture me no matter what I say.

"That's what I thought." And then his fingers brush against my bud again, but only that spot as he keeps me pressed against the wall. I can't focus on anything except where he's touching me. That intense rush spreads from my core throughout my body like wildfire—out of control.

And then he fucking stops—his fingers hover over me but not touching me.

I groan and arch my body off the wall, searching for his touch. My body is begging for him to touch me again, to let me finish.

"Are you not enjoying yourself, wife?"

I whimper. "Make me come."

"I thought you hated me? Why would you want me to make you come?"

And then his finger presses over my bud, causing me to gasp. I try to let myself come. I try to let go of the pressure building inside of me. I try to find my release, but he stops before I have a chance.

Again and again and fucking again, he touches me, bringing me right to the edge of a cliff before stopping abruptly—never letting me go over.

"Please," I beg again, with tears streaming down my face.

"Please, what? Let you come? Let you feel pleasure? I don't think you deserve any pleasure, do you?"

I'm losing it. He's pushed me too far, and I can't stand it much longer. I need a release. I need to get out of this basement. I need...

My body is worked up and flooded with built-up energy. Finally, the pressure bursts—just not in the enjoyable way.

I don't even know what I'm about to do when I do it. But I explode in a fury of emotion, wiggling free of Lennox's hold and grabbing the gun on his hip, and aiming it at his heart.

"Don't move."

I can feel him freeze, but he's not afraid of me. He's not afraid of anything, even death. Threatening to kill him won't do anything. He'll fight me every step.

This is a game, just a game. So play it, Rialta.

"Kneel." I pant, my body still worked up from his touch, still needing him to finish the job.

I take a step forward, until I'm right in front of him— the gun still aimed at his head.

"Push my pants down." I try to keep the tremor out of my voice, but I can't. I'm terrified of letting him touch me, but more terrified of him not.

His hands ease up to my waistband and carefully peel my pants down, his fingertips grazing every inch of skin as he lowers them to my ankles.

I swallow hard, considering my next move. It's not too late to turn back.

"What do you want me to do?" Lennox asks, his voice full of amusement at our predicament.

I press the gun against his temple, reminding him that he's no longer in control—I am.

He stops breathing, waiting for me to either blow his brains out or give him his order. He doesn't beg for me to spare his life. He doesn't say anything more. He lets me have control.

"Lick me, Lennox. Lick me until I tell you to stop. Eat my pussy until I come all over your face," I bark at him.

His hands find my hips in the dark, and then he presses his lips against my pussy, his tongue darting between my folds to taste me. I can barely make out his eyes in the darkness, and I swear I see a wicked gleam of approval at my choice to use my control against him.

I gasp as his tongue finally finds my clit. My body is so worked up that I could have come from that lick alone, but that would get him off too easy. And I want to savor this moment because it will most likely be the last time I let this man touch me in such an intimate way.

The gun stays pointed at his head, while my other hand tangles in his hair as he continues to lick just like I told him to. Over and over and over his tongue swoops through me, bringing me so close to exploding on his face, but I hold myself back.

I glance down at him, wishing I could see more of him. I wish I had had the sense to turn on the lights before I ordered him to lick me so I could see his expression as he makes me fall to pieces.

Is he enjoying himself? Is he pleased? Angry? Deviant?

He moans into my clit, rocking my body harder.

"Oh, fuck," I whisper.

He grins against my mound, answering my silent questions.

One of his hands slides down my hip to my inner thigh, until he's pressing two fingers at my entrance. I'm soaked, but he still tests how wet I am—teasing me before he pushes them both inside in one stroke.

I'm teetering on the edge. I need the release more than I need air. Yet, I don't let myself orgasm. I hold onto this feeling for as long as I can.

My hand holding the gun to his head falls to my side, while the other holds him firmly against my body. I try to memorize every moment so I can remember this when I'm with Andrea. Even if Andrea is the correct choice, Lennox is the better lover.

I memorize how his lips feel against my skin, how his fingers pull every bit of my wetness in and out of me. I memorize the sounds of his moans and growls, how his hair feels in my grip. I memorize how his eyes find a way to look up at me through the darkness—telling me so much in that fucking gaze.

Lennox fucks me with his fingers harder and faster, his tongue pressing deeper into my bud. A ferocious growl from his throat ripples from my core up to my chest, and I explode. My body trembles as the orgasm rips through me, flooding all my senses with Lennox.

Fucking Lennox. Sexy, annoying, relentless Lennox.

When my orgasm settles, forever etched into every muscle, nerve, and fiber, Lennox lets me go.

I inch a step away from him as he leans back on his ankles. Then I pull my pants back up.

I hold the gun at my side, knowing I don't have to point it at his head to get him to do what I want him to do.

"What now?" he asks.

I suck in a breath.

Now, I leave you forever. And then my plan will almost be complete.

I take a step back toward the stairs.

"Count to hundred, then you can get up," I say.

Then I disappear up the stairs before he can react. He won't follow. He's in too much shock at what just happened.

We're very evenly matched, him and me. We've both become villains to get what we want. Both forced the other to fuck, to do terrible, monstrous things. Both tried to tear the other apart, to ruin and break them.

I touch my finger to my lips, still tingling from his kisses. *Are we really villains when all we did was force the other to do things we wanted to do anyway? Things we enjoyed more than anything? Things we couldn't come up with a legitimate reason to do without being forced so we could keep our own agendas and pride?*

I grin.

Fuck, I'm screwed.

I open the basement door and am about to step out when I spot Gage's dark eyes staring at me from the living room.

Shit.

I freeze.

I could run, but if I do and Gage decides to follow, he'll shoot me dead before I get down the sidewalk. I still have my gun hidden on the other side of the door, but I won't run. I'll fight my way out if I have to.

But then Gage does something I'm not expecting from him. He takes a long moment to study me, really study me. He hates me. He wants me dead for what I've done to all of them. All of their loyalty has rightfully stayed with River, but his eyes soften when he sees me. It's as if he's looking at me for the first time.

He gives me the slightest of nods. My eyes widen when I

realize he's going to let me go. Maybe he thinks I'll be tortured more by waiting for them to find me. But I'm thankful, whatever the reason, so I disappear out the main door into the morning light.

CHAPTER 18

Lennox

I CAN'T CONTAIN my grin as I watch Rialta dart up the stairs, my gun at her side, and the glow around her from the orgasm I just gave her.

I sniff my fingers, breathing her in, before licking her juices clean off. God, it felt good to taste her again, to feel her quaking and moaning because of the pleasure I'm giving her. I didn't care that I was kneeling in a dark basement or that she had a gun pointed at my head. I knew she wasn't going to shoot me, even if she does still hate me.

But what is she up to?

And what is the truth?

I'm more confused by her than ever, while also more in love with her than ever.

I scrape my teeth over my bottom lip as my grin widens again at the strength she displayed. I called her selfish. I pushed her, trying to get answers. But she took control, and she claimed what she needed from me. I couldn't be prouder of her.

But I have no idea what I should do next.

I wait a few minutes in the basement, trying to think of a clue as to her intentions. Unfortunately, I come up empty.

I stand and creep up the stairs, unsure of what I'm going to find.

"She's gone," Gage says, making me jump when I open the basement door.

I nod.

I'm about to go check on Ri and Beckett when I stop and look at Gage, processing what he said.

"You saw her leave?" I ask.

"Yes."

I frown. "And you let her go?"

He stares at the door as if replaying the scene in his mind. "Yes."

He doesn't offer more of an explanation.

"Gage, please, we're on the same side. I know you think I'm blinded by my love for her, but I promise, I'm not going to make any more decisions that involve this family without talking to everyone first. Tell me what happened."

Gage's eyes flick back to me as he studies me carefully, trying to determine if he believes me or not. We've been through a lot together, but he's grown closer to Beckett over the last few months, while I've grown closer to Hayes. But that doesn't mean I don't love him like a brother, and I know he loves me the same. We've been through far too much together.

"I could have shot her, killed her if I wanted to. I could have forced her to stay, or at the very least, gone after her," Gage says.

"Why didn't you?"

"She had a gun. She saw me first. She should have shot me on the spot. She knows I don't trust her anymore. My loyalty lies with this family over her. She has an agenda, and I could have stopped her. But she didn't shoot me. And I don't understand why."

I drop my lips, as confused as he is about her actions.

"You don't understand why what?" Hayes asks as he walks into the living room. Sun is beginning to pour in, pushing out all the darkness from the night before.

"I don't understand Rialta's agenda. I don't understand whose side she's on. I don't understand if she's trained or lucky or just brave enough to fool us into thinking she is skilled with a weapon when she's really not. I don't know if she loves Lennox, or Kit, or Andrea. I don't know if she cares about Ri or caused her injuries. I don't know if she cares about any of us. I don't know if she's working for her father or some enemy," Gage answers, but then pauses. "But there was something in her gaze before she left that begged me to trust her. That I needed to let her go, so I did."

"That was foolish," Beckett says, making us all jump. None of us realized he walked down the hallway.

"Ri's sleeping, and I heard you talking about Rialta," Beckett explains.

I nod. "I've made mistakes when it comes to Rialta, and if it caused the loss to your family and pain to Ri, then I'll forever be sorry. I won't make that mistake again. But before I take any actions when it comes to Rialta, I want to know everyone's opinions."

Beckett's eyes are swollen and red. His skin is pale, and sweat soaks his hair. His clothes are covered in Ri's blood. We all need a shower and a good night's sleep. We all need time to process everything that's happened.

But time is never something we have to spend as our own. We have a job to do.

"What do you think, Beckett?" I ask.

"We have evidence that Rialta worked with Andrea to take Ri. Ri was pregnant, and Rialta hadn't been able to get pregnant yet. Vincent considers Ri his second daughter, so if Rialta never had a child, our child would become Vincent's heir. Andrea couldn't have that, and Rialta went along with it. She helped him figure out how to kidnap Ri, and then Andrea tortured her until there was no longer a threat," Beckett's voice is calm and steady, hiding the pain he's going to live with the rest of his life.

They will be able to try again, but he'll never forgive himself for not protecting Ri and his baby. But it's impossible to have a baby in this world and guarantee their safety. It's a fear they've had this entire time. It's why they were happy when I agreed to marry Rialta and offer her my protection instead of them worrying about her safety too.

There are a lot of flaws with Beckett's theory. The biggest being that Rialta couldn't get pregnant because she was pregnant. Ri's baby wasn't a threat. And despite spending a lot of their life apart, Ri and Rialta love each other. So it would take a lot for one of them to betray the other. I'm not sure if Rialta actually betrayed Ri or just trusted the wrong person with her sister's life.

But I'm not the one who should dispute Beckett's story. And I'm not telling anyone that Rialta is pregnant, especially after what happened to Ri. I don't know whose child it is—Kit's, Andrea's, or mine, but I do know the child is Rialta's, and I will protect any child of Rialta's with my life.

"Do you still think Rialta should be trusted, Gage? That her motives are pure and innocent?" Beckett stares at his closest friend.

"I'm an analytical man. I only make decisions with the facts. And the facts seem to support your theory, Beckett."

"Thank you. So that's two votes against Rialta," Beckett says.

"However..." Gage rises from the couch and paces back and forth, staring at the ground as he replays everything in his head. Finally, he stops. "However, there was something in her look that is going to haunt me. There is a lot she's not telling us. I saw how Ri and her were together. They loved each other. So something huge had to have changed for Rialta to have harmed Ri, and I can't figure out what that would be."

"So, how do you vote?" Beckett barks.

Gage looks at me and then sighs. "I'm on your side, Beckett."

Beckett smirks and raises his eyebrows as he looks at Hayes, waiting for him to weigh in.

Hayes wipes his glasses on the hem of his shirt, stalling.

"Hayes?" I ask.

Hayes puts his glasses back on and then looks from Beckett to me. "I agree with Gage— Rialta is hiding something. And as I'm the positive one of the group and always sees the best in people—I'm not going to condemn her without a fair trial. No matter how horrible the crime. So I vote to trust Rialta for now."

All eyes fall to me—the only expression I care about, though, is Beckett's. His devastation is marked across his face. I know how he wants me to vote. And there is a part of me that thinks I owe him after what happened to Ri. I don't want to lose his friendship, but I can't vote the way he wants me to.

He shakes his head incredulously before I even speak.

"I love her. I can't vote against her without undeniable proof, and there are too many holes in this story that don't make sense."

"What are you going to do, then? The vote is split," Gage asks.

I sigh. "I'm going to wait for Ri to wake up—she'll be the tiebreaker."

"You might be waiting a while. She's still unconscious.

The doctor thinks she suffered a concussion on top of everything else. And that sometimes when you experience that level of trauma, the body shuts down and sleeps to avoid reality," Beckett says.

"I'll wait, however long it takes," I answer.

"What are we going to do about Kit?" Hayes asks.

"Keep him alive and protected. Hopefully, we can jog his memory about who took him," I answer.

"I'll make some breakfast for everyone," Hayes says, heading to the kitchen.

"I'll go check on Kit," Gage says.

Suddenly, it's just Beckett and me left.

"I'm sorry. I love Ri—she's like a sister to me. I'd do anything to protect her, and if anything changes about who took her, who hurt her, then I'll do everything I can to get revenge for her. You know that," I say.

Beckett stares down the hallway to where his wife sleeps. "I know you do, but your love has blinded you." He turns and looks at me. "Just like it blinded me."

I furrow my brow.

Beckett smiles softly, like he's remembering a sweet memory. "Love does strange things to us. I don't fault you for defending the woman you love—I'm just trying to give you some advice. I lucked out that the woman I fell for was worth it in the end. I'm not sure yet if Rialta is worth it, but my wife is. And if I or the others have to choose—we'll choose Ri."

"As you should."

"But you'll choose Rialta."

I swallow, not wanting to say it out loud.

"I don't want us to be on different sides, but you know something you aren't telling us," he says.

I nod.

He raises his eyebrows, waiting for me to elaborate.

"I can't tell you everything, but I will say that your theory about Rialta is incorrect."

Beckett narrows his eyes, studying me closely before finally nodding.

I still don't know what I'm going to do about Rialta. I need Ri to wake up—to tell us all what happened. To tell me what to do about Rialta because I'm hopeless when it comes to her. Ri's the only one who can give me evidence that Rialta is actually as cruel as she appears.

CHAPTER 19

Rialta

"RIALTA? WHAT ARE YOU DOING HERE?" Vincent asks, his eyes wide in disbelief from behind his desk. His guards didn't warn him. I snuck past them without anyone seeing me.

The guys haven't tracked me yet.

Andrea doesn't know.

No one knows I'm here.

I need to have a conversation with Vincent before anyone else tries to influence my decision.

"We need to talk," I say, closing the door behind me.

His eyes rake up and down my body, quickly looking for any sign of injury.

"I'm fine," I say, walking toward the chair across from his desk.

Vincent stands, meeting me before I take a seat. I walk without fear, like I'm in control of my own destiny, not like I'm here to beg my father for permission on how I'm to spend the rest of my life.

He places his hands on my shoulders, assessing me again.

"I'm not hurt," I try again.

"Thank god for that." He pulls me into a hug, and I swear I feel a tear fall down his cheek and onto my shoulder. I've rarely seen him cry. I wasn't expecting this reaction.

"What did you think happened to me?" I lean back, looking him in his soaked eyes.

He shakes his head. "You talk first. It's clear I've been misinformed."

I frown as I sink into one of the chairs. He sits in the one next to me, instead of back behind his desk like usual. This feels more personal, more like a father and daughter instead of the usual business arrangement.

"Tell me everything," he says.

I shake my head. "I don't have time to tell you everything, nor do you deserve to hear everything."

He winces at my words.

"But I've made my decision about who I want to spend the rest of my life with."

He stares at me with deep sorrow etched into his face. "If it was only about who your husband is, the choice would always be yours. But it's more than that; it's about which man can keep you alive. Which man can run my empire, keep my men in line, and use them to protect the Corsi line forever."

I purse my lips. After everything, I'm still not sure I'm going to be able to convince him of anything.

"I chose Lennox for you, but it's clear he's betrayed you. You want that marriage annulled and him killed. Andrea has said as much. I still think Lennox is the best man for the job. But I know you came here to persuade me otherwise."

"I did." I take a deep breath. "I want to marry Andrea. I want you to make him your successor."

Vincent stands, walking to the window. He knew this was coming, but I'm not sure why he's reacting this way. I don't speak more. I don't explain my reasoning. I wait for him to come to me, hoping he'll end up revealing some of his motivations and reasoning.

Finally, Vincent turns and looks at me. He's breathing deeply, his nostrils flaring with each breath, and he's trying to keep his cool.

"I think you're making the wrong decision, but it's a decision I will let you make. But my rules apply the same for him as they did for Lennox. He must kill the man who has been hurting our family for years, and he must prove his love to you by producing an heir within a year, or my men will kill him."

A small smile spreads across my lips. "Thank you."

He frowns at my reaction. "I'll grant your annulment from Lennox if that's what you want. You can be married to Andrea as soon as it can be arranged."

I nod, knowing what's coming next and hoping I'll be able to stop him.

"I'll send a team of men to eliminate Lennox, and the annulment will be done."

"No," I breathe out.

"What?"

"I don't want you to kill Lennox."

"It isn't up to you, dear. He and I made an arrangement —one in blood that my entire team witnessed. They will hold him to his vow. He has to die for not fulfilling it."

I shake my head. "There has to be another way."

Vincent narrows his eyes at me in the way he does when he's commanding answers from me.

But I don't back down. I've grown a lot through this experience. I'm not the naive princess everyone thinks I am. I'm strong enough to win this battle against anyone.

"Why don't you want Lennox dead? You're choosing another man to be your husband. And my understanding is that Lennox killed your former lover..."

"His name is Kit."

Vincent nods. "That's right, Kit. He killed Kit. He hurt you. I understand why you want to get rid of him. But why can't I eliminate him?"

"Because *I* want to."

Vincent's eyebrows jump up, and his face pales as he looks at me. He realizes I'm no longer his clean-handed daughter. I'm fully capable of spilling blood when I need to.

I press my lips together and stare Vincent down, waiting for him to show the same appreciation that he does with River. He loves how strong she is. He loves how she can shoot better than any man and defend herself just as easily. I'm waiting for him to tell me how proud of me he is.

He sinks into the chair next to me and takes my hands into his lap, rubbing over the top of my hands with his thumbs. He doesn't speak.

"I thought that's what you always wanted from me. You wanted me to be able to protect myself like River can. I don't understand why you're disappointed in me," I say.

His head snaps up, and there's pain in his eyes. "No, I'm not disappointed in you. I could never be disappointed in you."

"What then?"

"I'm disappointed in myself, in how marvelously I have failed you."

"You haven't failed me. You've kept me safe. You sent me away to save me. And you found me a husband to protect me. But I don't need anyone's protection anymore. I'll agree to the husband I believe is the best man for the job, not because I need his protection."

Vincent shakes his head again. "But you shouldn't have ever had to get your hands bloody. I promised your mother that I would never let this life take hold of you in that way.

Now that you've experienced bloodshed like that, you won't ever be able to escape it."

"I'm strong enough to handle it."

"I know—I know you are. I just didn't want this for you. I tried to keep you from this, and I failed."

There's a knock on the door. Vincent stands and walks toward it. He cracks the door and speaks to one of his men on the other side before closing it again and facing me.

"I have a meeting I need to take. I'll be gone two hours, three tops. We can continue this conversation when I get back, but I'm not sure I can honor your request. If you want an annulment, then Lennox must die. And I'm not sure the men will wait for you to be the one to do it. And many of my men distrust Andrea, so it will be an uphill battle to make him my replacement."

"I'm pregnant," I blurt out.

Vincent freezes. He doesn't congratulate me the way he did River. He doesn't get excited that he finally has an heir to pass everything to. He doesn't ask whose baby it is. He doesn't say anything in response at all.

He just walks out the door without another word, leaving me alone with my thoughts.

And I have a lot of thoughts as I head back to my old room. I end up falling asleep on my bed, eventually waking to an anxious knock at the door.

"Come in," I say drowsily.

The door opens, and one of Vincent's men enters. "I'm sorry to bother you, Rialta, but..."

"Spit it out."

"Vincent's been shot."

CHAPTER 20

Lennox

"I MADE COFFEE AND OMELETS," Hayes says, carrying a tray into Ri's room. "But no one will eat any of the omelets, even though we should."

He starts passing out coffee and plates of eggs. Beckett takes his coffee cup but immediately places his plate on the end table beside Ri's bed. Gage politely holds his plate in his lap, and he begins to down his coffee. And I hold mine in each hand as I sit in a chair on the other side of Ri. Hayes takes a seat in a chair next to Gage near the foot of the bed.

This has been the arrangement for three days. We all brought chairs in, and we've been staying vigilant around Ri. She hasn't opened her eyes or done much other than breathe since we brought her here.

The doctor checks in twice a day. She said there's nothing physically wrong with her. She performed a small surgery to clean out her uterus and make sure she doesn't get an infection. The rest of her wounds are beginning to heal. She just said these things take time.

Beckett sets his coffee down, so he can hold her hand

again. The IV tubing swings as he knocks it before taking her hand in his. It's the only sound in the room.

None of us know what to do—we are all so hopeless when it comes to Ri. And we have no idea how to help her.

I stare down at the eggs on my plate. The only way I know how to help is to take care of everyone. I set my coffee on the end table, and I start eating. Slowly, I force each bite into my mouth. My stomach curls as the first bite hits it, and I realize how badly I need food, how much we all do.

I look to Hayes. He takes no convincing to start digging into his food.

Gage takes a harsher look, but he eventually takes a few bites.

Beckett is going to take more swaying.

"Eat a couple of bites, Beckett," I say.

He shakes his head.

"For Ri. She's going to wake up soon, and you're going to need your strength."

Beckett frowns, his eyes flicking around the room—looking each of us in the eyes. Finally, he rolls his eyes and shoves a couple of quick bites of egg in his mouth, not even bothering to use a fork. But it satisfies us all.

Then we all go back to sipping our coffees and watching Ri's chest rise and fall with each breath, hoping this is the breath she opens her eyes.

We down three more coffees by midafternoon. None of us have slept in days. Our eyes are bloodshot, our hands jittery, but all of us refuse to sleep more than a quick nod off in these chairs.

"Oh my god," Hayes says, barely able to get the words out.

Ri's eyes flicker open. I've never seen a better sight than seeing her open her eyes.

Beckett collapses on top of her, while Hayes, Gage, and I stand up—walking to the edge of the bed.

We each take turns hugging her or squeezing her hand before filing out of the room to give Beckett and her some privacy.

"I'm going to make something for everyone to eat," Hayes says with a large grin.

"Are you always thinking about food?" Gage asks.

"Always," Hayes grins.

Gage rolls his eyes, but he smiles as Hayes hops off to the kitchen. Then Gage turns his expression to me. "How are you feeling?"

I frown. "I'm fine."

"Your injuries are healing?"

I ignore the burning that runs down my spine with every step, the ache in my back, and the shooting pains every time I move. I've been taking antibiotics to prevent infection, but I've given up on the pain pills. The pain is going to be with me for a long time.

"Yes."

Gage can see through me, but he doesn't say anything. "Have you given any more thought about Rialta?"

I shake my head. "I've been trying not to think about her until Ri wakes up. Now that she has, I'll have a conversation with her soon."

Gage looks off in the distance, and I can tell he has more on his mind.

"What is it?"

He sighs. "I've been watching Rialta's movements these last few days. Do you want to know?"

Do I want to know? Hell yes, I want to know.

"No, not until after I talk to Ri."

He nods. "Just remember you used to be enemies."

"What's that supposed to mean? That we still should be? Or that enemies eventually become allies?"

Gage doesn't answer; he just walks away.

Strange.

We don't continue our conversation even while him, Hayes, and I eat together. We offer Kit to eat with us, but he prefers to stay in his room. He knows Rialta left, but he doesn't know why or when she'll be back. Beckett hasn't left Ri's room, even after Hayes brought them something to eat. It's understandable, considering all the emotions they have to process. Despite Ri being awake, all of our moods grow solemn again as we realize the loss they are feeling.

I know they can try again, but I'm not sure they're going to want to until they can find a way out of this life. So they either lose their dream of having kids, or we lose them in our lives.

Suddenly, the door to Ri's bedroom swings open, and Beckett steps out. His face is a contrast of emotions—happiness, sadness, guilt, shame, relief, and pain. He feels it all. But above everything, he looks absolutely exhausted.

"Lennox, Ri wants to see you."

I stand, taking a deep breath, trying to prepare myself for how hard this is going to be. I walk down the hallway to Beckett. He eyes me, telling me to help her, to help them both. Because he can't help her.

I squeeze his shoulder. I can't promise anyone anything. If cheering up is needed, Hayes is a much better choice. Gage could give her information from any surveillance he's done. I'm not sure what I can offer her that would help, but I'll do my best.

As much as I want to ask her about how she would vote on Ri, I know today isn't the day to burden her with that question. So it will have to wait another day. My chest grips my heart at that thought. I'm not sure I can bare it.

"Are you coming?" I ask Beckett.

He shakes his head. "No, she wants to talk to you alone."

I nod. "Then take a shower or a nap. Do something to take care of yourself. You'll be able to help her more once you get some rest."

His lips thin into a frown, and then he leaves me to enter Ri's room alone. I'm not sure if he's going to take my advice or not.

I enter the room quietly, not sure if Ri's going to be awake or asleep. I close the door carefully, and then I find her gaze.

She smiles at me like I'm her favorite person in the world, but that's Ri. When you're with her, she makes you feel like she loves you.

I plaster a nervous smile on my face as I walk toward the side of her bed and lean down to give her a gentle hug. Her warmth wraps around me, and her hand strokes my back like I'm the one in need of comforting. Our hug ends, and I ease into the chair next to her bed.

I open my mouth to ask her how she's doing but snap it shut, instantly realizing it's a stupid question.

"I'm okay," she says with assurance in her voice.

I look past the shield she's putting up.

"No, you're not."

Her shoulders slump, and her façade fades away. "No, I'm not fine," her voice quakes.

I wrap my arms around her again as her tears fall onto my shoulder, wetting my shirt. She almost immediately tries to stop the tears.

"Don't—get it all out," I say.

She continues trying to stop until I let all of my own pain and loss out, too, through my own tears. Finally, she releases every painful emotion—I feel them all. And she feels mine, even though neither of us know any details.

Together we process. Wave after wave bursts through us. Every time one of us begins to slow, the other starts up again. I don't think I've ever cried this much in my life.

"Okay, I don't think I have any tears left to cry," Ri croaks out between hiccups.

I hiccup too.

And we both smile—a tiny spark of genuine happiness in both of our expressions. Not enough to live off of, but enough that we can stop crying.

I grab two tissues from the end table and hand one to her. We both blow our noses, but it's no use. The crying has made both of our noses stuffy and our faces swollen. But the crying session was worth it for the calm release we're both feeling now.

"Can I get you anything?" I ask.

"Yes, conversation."

I nod and sit down on the chair next to her bed.

"I'm sorry about breaking down on you. I know you've been through a lot recently, but you're the only one who can understand my pain and loss. And I couldn't cry with Beckett." It's clear that Beckett has shared some of my past with her if she thinks that.

"Why not?" I ask.

"I don't want Beckett to see how much this hurts me. I don't want him to blame himself. And if I started crying with him, I probably wouldn't stop."

"You should show him how you're feeling. He needs to cry too."

"He did, but I couldn't," she says.

I close my mouth, knowing it's not my place to give her advice. She loves Beckett, and they each have to mourn in different ways, but I just hope they don't drift apart. Their love for each other is strong, but even the best relationships struggle to handle a loss like this. Especially when it wasn't just chance that took their baby from them.

We sit in comfortable silence for a few minutes. "The others are anxious to see you. Hayes can cheer you up, and Gage would be happy to share intel when you're ready to hear it. And I'm sure Beckett is anxious to come check on you."

Ri's eyes glaze over. "I know."

"You can talk to me about anything."

"So can you."

"I don't want to burden you with anything."

"Ask me—ask me how I feel about Rialta. Ask me how I'd vote. Don't wait any longer. I know you think you have time, and that my grief is more important than going after Rialta, but it's not. Ask me. I'm not fragile. I won't break. I'm the same woman I've always been. I'm strong—I'll recover from this. And so will you. Ask me."

I swallow hard, not sure I'm ready. Maybe that's why I haven't asked because I'm afraid of the answer. I'm terrified that Rialta really is the enemy. I'm scared shitless that I'm going to have to hunt her down and kill her for what she did to Ri.

"Is Rialta the love of my life or my enemy?"

CHAPTER 21

Rialta

VINCENT'S OFFICE makes up the entire basement of the safe house. There are no windows, just bulletproof walls and a single door to enter and exit. Half a dozen guards are stationed outside the door. It's the safest place he can be. The room used to serve as just a safe bunker where he could meet with his men, but after he was shot, a bed, kitchenette, and basic necessities were moved down here to make him more comfortable.

I enter with Andrea by my side. I called him as soon as I found out Vincent was shot. I knew I'd need him to help me handle Vincent and the men until he woke back up. He's been unconscious for three days. Today is the first day he's been awake, and of course, he's choosing to sit in his leather executive chair behind his desk.

"You should be in bed," I say as I walk down the stairs.

"There is too much to be done to sleep," Vincent says.

I let go of Andrea's arm and walk over to Vincent, kissing him on the cheek. "It's good to see you up. You gave us all quite a scare."

Vincent's silent as he looks from me to Andrea.

"It's good to see you doing so well. I've been doing my best to keep everything going in the meantime. And everything points to this attack being The Abyss," Andrea says.

"The Abyss?" Vincent asks.

Andrea nods. "Yes, sir. It's the name we've come up with in connection to the man who has been taking out everyone in your family."

Vincent narrows his eyes at Andrea. I'm not sure if he likes him or hates him, but he's one of his men. So Vincent respects him as one of his minions over which he has absolute power.

"How are you feeling?" I ask, trying to draw the focus back to what's important. I'm not sure if Vincent is going to thank Andrea for the information or try to fight him for coming here with his daughter like I'm already his.

"Good as ever."

I stare at him. "Really? How are you feeling? You were shot in the side three days ago. You can't be feeling good as ever."

"I'm fine, daughter. I'm just anxious to get you settled and an heir in place." The way he looks at me tells me I've overcomplicated things. He's disappointed I didn't just stay married to Lennox. I'm choosing another man. I'm pregnant, and he has no clue whose baby it is. I'm a huge disappointment.

I step back to the other side of the desk and lean into Andrea's side as he hooks an arm over my shoulders.

"Let her go," a deep voice says from behind us.

We don't have to look behind us to know that a gun is pointed at Andrea. He looks down at me and winks—he's confident he can take the man out.

But who is it? And how did they get past Vincent's guards?

Andrea doesn't let me go—in fact, he pulls me to him tighter and then turns around quickly. He pulls his gun out and pushes me behind him, putting himself between me and the gun pointed at us.

Both men fire.

Both men miss.

And then I realize who the intruder is.

"Kit?" I whisper.

I have no idea how he's standing, let alone where he got a gun, or how he got down here.

Before Kit responds, guards file down the stairs at the sound of gunfire, and Andrea scoops me up into his arms. He carries me back behind the desk at the same time Vincent ducks down behind it.

Vincent looks me up and down, assuring himself that I'm unharmed. And then he gives a nod of gratitude to Andrea.

My heart beats a million miles an hour—Kit. He couldn't have survived everything to be killed now.

I hear more gunfire.

"No!" I cry out.

I try to peek around the desk, but Andrea holds me tightly, keeping me from looking.

"No!" I scream again. "Let me go!"

I fight against Andrea's grasp, but his hands tighten their hold; combined with Vincent grabbing my arm, I have no chance of breaking free. No chance of stopping this. No chance of saving Kit. After everything I've done to protect him—my first love, the father of my baby.

"Please," I beg. "Kit's innocent. Don't let him die."

Andrea looks to Vincent, letting him make the decision.

With the tiniest of nods, Vincent gives Andrea permission. Andrea grabs something from his pocket —handcuffs.

My eyes widen—*no*.

He slaps one on my wrist and the other to the desk

before he darts around the desk, as does Vincent—leaving me trapped to the desk.

Fucking sociopaths.

I growl and try to yank on the handcuffs, but I'm stuck. I can't do anything but hope and pray that Kit is going to be okay.

I hear a scuffle, more shots, and then finally, silence.

I can't move far, but I can ease my head around the side of the desk enough to make out most of the scene.

There are several guards down. But Vincent, Andrea, and Kit are all alive. And they are all pointing their guns at each other.

"Don't shoot," I cry out.

They all turn and look at me—none of them knowing who I'm referring to.

Andrea tries to take a step toward Kit, but Vincent speaks first. "Enough."

His voice is booming, echoing through the room.

Vincent looks from man to man to me. Like he's finally piecing together a puzzle. "Lennox, I know you're here."

I stare around the room in confusion but see Lennox walk out of the shadows in the corner of the room—a slit of a door left open behind him. Apparently, there is more than one door leading into this room. Now that I think about it, Vincent usually prefers a house with secret tunnels underneath, so I shouldn't be surprised.

But I am surprised to see Lennox here.

He doesn't pull out his gun like the others. His eyes just cut to me with lava-bubbling rage before he looks back to the circle of men.

"Lower your weapons—both of you," Vincent says.

Kit and Andrea immediately lower their guns.

When Vincent is satisfied, he holsters his gun.

"Now, I've had enough of this. We are going to settle

this once and for all." Vincent glares at each of the men, driving the fear of god into all of them. There is no sign of recently being shot in his stance, no pain etched on his face—just pure fury beating down on all of us.

"All three of you think you are the best for my daughter. Lennox—I gave you the job, and so far, you've failed. Rialta wants nothing to do with you. Kit—you think my daughter loves you, but it's just puppy love that comes from being her first. It's not real, and you don't have the skills to keep her safe, no matter how convincing you tried to be coming to her rescue. And Andrea—you may have the skills to protect her, but you're a power-hungry ass. You care more about replacing me than my daughter."

Vincent looks to me with an exhausted look.

I shake my head in frustration. *Don't do this,* my eyes beg. *Let me make my own choice, please.*

Vincent sighs, but his eyes glow with rage.

"None of you are good enough for Rialta. All of you are fools in your own ways. But I'm getting older, and as much as I try, I won't live forever. Eventually, The Abyss or someone else will finally succeed in killing me, and I need to know my family line is taken care of. I need to know Rialta and her children will survive. The Corsi family will continue forever."

Vincent walks toward me, looking at me intently. If he's trying to tell me something, I have no idea what it is. He turns and leans on the desk, turning to face the three men.

"I'm tired of the three of you fighting for my daughter. So I'm proposing a final challenge. It's the same challenge I gave to Lennox, and he's failed to fulfill. You have three tasks you have to complete in order to win the right to ask Rialta to be yours forever. She can still say no, though, even if you complete all three tasks and are the rightful winner."

My eyebrows shoot up at the power he's giving me.

"So I would consider if you will be able to convince Rialta to be your partner forever before you decide to enter. The three tasks you must complete are to kill The Abyss, prove to me you love Rialta, and then produce an heir within a year of her agreeing to be yours."

Vincent stares each of them down one at a time—Andrea, Kit, and Lennox.

"Whoever completes the tasks first, wins. But you must achieve all three."

There's a charge about the room—of anticipation of Vincent's final declaration.

"You must choose now if you will compete or surrender now. If you surrender, you can walk out that door, and no one here will think about you again. No one will go after you. You will be free to live out the rest of your life in peace."

He pauses for dramatic effect.

"But if you decide to compete, then realize you're taking the same blood oath Lennox took when he agreed to marry my daughter. If you win, you get a chance with my daughter. If you fail, you die."

CHAPTER 22

Lennox

I SHOULD BE tired of Vincent's games, but I get why he does it. Rialta lives without fear. She's so free and willing to risk everything just to enjoy life. She doesn't hide away in fear of a man hunting her down one day. And so that's how she chooses her relationships.

I know the torment Vincent felt losing his family. I've experienced the same thing. I know what it's like to lose everything. And yet, his experience is different. Because he didn't lose everything—he still has his daughter. And he'll do anything to protect her, even hold these games to determine the best man for the job.

But he gave Rialta more power this time. She gets the ultimate say. I suspect he thinks once only one of us remains, she'll accept him as her husband. I understand Vincent's need to protect her and her children as best as he can, but this plan is going to backfire on him.

I stare at Rialta, still handcuffed to the back of the desk, her head barely able to peek around it. My blood boils at the thought of her forced into that position.

"Who agrees to enter my game?" Vincent asks.

"I do," Kit says without hesitation.

"I do," Andrea says a second later.

Rialta's eyes are wide with fear. *She's scared for someone's life, but whose? Kit's?*

"I do," I say.

"Very well. May the best man win," Vincent says.

Kit jumps forward the second Vincent finishes his sentence. "I'd like to make a declaration of love. I love your daughter very much, Mr. Corsi. I've loved her since I was fifteen years old. You may call that puppy love—the kind you realize years later wasn't real love. You may say she's just the first person to ever show me attention, the first girl I kissed, but my love for her has only grown.

"I haven't grown up in this dangerous world like the others. I've only recently learned how to use a gun. I don't know a thing about running a criminal organization. It's not my life calling—but I'd give up any dreams I have to marry Rialta. I'll never stop loving her, and I know she still loves me. She's been trying to protect me by pushing me away, but I'll have no life if it's not with her. I know you think I can't protect her or keep her safe, but I'm a fast learner. And I'd risk my own life to keep her alive every time."

"Are you finished?" Vincent asks, amusement in his voice.

Kit stutters, confused why his speech didn't seem to sway Vincent.

"No, I declared my love, which checks one of the tasks off the list. I can check off the second as well," Kit continues.

Both Andrea and my eyes snap to Kit. He couldn't have killed The Abyss.

"Rialta's pregnant with my baby," Kit says.

My heart stops. I already knew it, but I'm not sure how he found out. He must have overheard us talking or guessed as much. A charge surges through the room as everyone takes that information in and processes it differently.

I should surrender now and keep my life. Maybe Rialta would let me play uncle to their child or help with her security team since I wouldn't trust Kit to ever figure that out.

But there is a dark, twisted thought in the back of my mind that doesn't care about the pregnancy. Ri was pregnant, too, and she lost the baby. The same thing could happen to Rialta. It's not a finished task until the baby is born. And there's always a chance that Rialta is wrong about the child's father. There's still a tiny chance that I could be the father.

"Kill The Abyss, and I'll consider your words then," Vincent says.

Suddenly, Andrea fires a shot at Kit.

My eyes stay on Vincent—seeing if he's going to put a stop to it. But he seems to not care if we fight it out or not. In his mind, only the strongest survives if we fight.

Kit aims his gun back, and I head toward Rialta—now's my chance to get her out of here. Once she's safe, I can figure out what to do. My only thought is getting her out of those handcuffs. The only time I want to see her in handcuffs is in my bed.

I take a step toward her when I feel a bullet whiz past my head. But the look in Rialta's eyes and her high-pitched scream keeps me locked on her.

I'm still moving to Rialta, but the change to kill Andrea is too tempting. Grinning like an idiot, I turn my own gun and shoot Andrea in the shoulder. But then I'm tackled, and my head hits the ground hard, the room going black.

When I come to, the room is empty.

Fuck.

I run out of the house in time to see Kit running

through the fields behind the house and Andrea driving a car down the drive.

I have two choices, two men to follow—Kit or Andrea. I assume Rialta is with Andrea, so my instinct is to follow them. But he won't hurt her. He needs her alive and to ultimately choose him if he succeeds in killing The Abyss.

Although my feet want to carry me toward her, I force my legs in the other direction—toward Kit.

CHAPTER 23

Lennox

WATCHING Kit run through the forest, I can't tell if he's hiding his skills or if he's just a fucking idiot. Either way, I need to catch up to him. As I start running, a car engine speeds off in the night. It takes all of my willpower to not turn around and go after that car.

I focus on my target—running as fast as I can. I'm not sure it's enough as the terrain turns from fields to forest. There are plenty of places for Kit to hide in this brush, and I'm not as fast as I once was. My injuries have slowed me down.

But I'm smarter than Kit. I'm not even sure he realizes I'm following him.

I eye the path he's taking, and I dart left—taking a shortcut. A moment later, I'm tackling him to the ground.

Kit immediately starts fighting, trying to wrestle him off of me. He almost succeeds, but I pin him under my weight just as Gage and Hayes show up.

"Finally," I sigh at them.

"Sorry, we wanted to see if you were still capable of taking someone down yourself," Hayes teases.

I roll my eyes, and Gage just shrugs his shoulders. Then the two of them help me and Kit up, while Gage aims his gun at Kit.

"Let's talk," I say to Kit.

Kit eyes the gun. "Seems like I'm at your mercy, so talk."

I sigh. "I'm trying to help you."

"Like you helped me by sticking me in a bedroom at your house and keeping me in the dark about what's going on? That didn't help me."

"No, like how I stitched you up, got you medical care, got you food, and protected you from harm." I glare at him.

His eyes shoot daggers back.

"I want you to win," I say. I can feel Gage and Hayes's eyes cut to me in confusion.

Kit narrows his eyes at me in suspicion. "Why? You're in love with her. It's clear to see. Why would you want me to win?"

"It's because I love her." My words settle before I continue. "And Rialta loves you. She still hates me. She would never choose me. I'm not sure she wants me to die anymore, but I do know she wants you to live."

"I'll never trust you," Kit says.

"Then you're signing your own death certificate," I snap back.

Kit stares off into the forest, as if he's considering running despite having a gun aimed at him and knowing the three of us would chase him down in a heartbeat.

"You've completed two of the three tasks. You've declared your love for her, and you've fathered her baby."

"So it's true? The baby really is mine?"

"That's not for me to say. What matters is that she loves you and wants to marry you, not me. And I want to help you."

"Why didn't you surrender when you had the chance? Why risk your life when you aren't even trying to compete for yourself?" Kit asks.

"I'm technically married to Rialta. I doubt Vincent or anyone else would let me live, even if I dropped out. And, because I love her. I'd do anything for her, including dying if I have to."

"You're not going to die," Gage says, surprising me with his insistence.

No one else says anything.

"It doesn't matter if Rialta loves me; I'll never be able to complete the final task. I don't know who The Abyss is, and even if I did, I'm sure he's far more skilled than I am," Kit says.

"That's where we come in. We'll help you find and kill him. We'll help you win," I say.

"Even if I believed you, I don't believe you are going to find and kill The Abyss. You haven't been able to all this time."

"We're going back to the Retribution Kings. They have resources that can help us find The Abyss," Hayes says.

"And we can use their men to help ensure Lennox survives this. Our only ask in exchange for helping you is that when you become the heir and take over Vincent's job, the Corsi men and Retribution Kings will become allies instead of enemies," Gage says.

We all stare at Kit, waiting for his response. He looks each of us in the eyes carefully. Finally, he says, "It doesn't seem I have a choice. It doesn't mean I trust you, any of you, but we have a deal."

Gage lowers his gun, and we all shake on it. I don't like Gage and Hayes going back to the Retribution Kings. I don't know what punishments they will have to endure to gain their trust again or even if they will take them back. But I know we don't have a choice.

We are all risking our lives in different ways. But I meant what I said—if it comes down to it, I'll die to give Rialta everything she wants and deserves. If she loves Kit, if she chooses him, then I have no problem dying for her.

CHAPTER 24

Rialta

"YOU'RE SAFE HERE," Andrea says as we step into a one-bedroom shack in the middle of the woods.

"I'm not safe anywhere," I say matter-of-factly back.

He frowns at me but doesn't argue.

If there's any electricity in this small cabin, he doesn't bother to turn it on. Instead, he uses the light from his phone to check things out. I can only see where he points the light—a small dingy couch, a fridge, and a microwave sit in a two-cabinet kitchen, and a queen bed sits in the far corner. I don't see another door.

"Does this place even have a bathroom?" I ask.

"It has an outhouse."

My eyes widen as my nose wrinkles in disgust. Then I realize an outhouse is a convenient excuse to escape. *But escape to where?* There's nowhere for me to go. We're in the middle of fucking nowhere.

"Why'd you bring me here?"

"Because it's safe. It's my personal safe house. No one knows about this place—not even my men. Not Vincent, no one. We're as safe as humanly possible," he says.

"You're not going to be able to find The Abyss from here."

"I'm not worried about The Abyss. I'm worried about the other two tasks."

I frown and swallow hard, trying to push my anxiety down.

He studies me head to toe. "But that's something we can discuss tomorrow. We should eat something and sleep."

He starts walking toward the door with his phone light. "I need to go turn on the electricity. I'll be right back. Make yourself at home."

And then Andrea is outside. I can hear his boots crunching leaves and twigs outside as he rounds the small cabin.

My heart pounds in my chest. I don't know what to do, but I need to get out of here. I need to figure out how to keep everyone I love alive, but my father's new terms put a damper on my original plan.

This might be my only chance.

I slip out the door, intent on running as soon as I can creep far enough away that he can't hear my footsteps.

I take one step, then another, then another. Each step is carefully placed, so Andrea doesn't realize I'm outside.

"The outhouse is on the other side," Andrea's voice booms.

Fuck.

My heart sinks. I turn and nod before heading in the outhouse's direction.

When I finish in the outhouse, Andrea is standing just outside. Cool breeze chills my cheek, as does his icy stare.

"I wanted to make sure you didn't get lost in the dark," he says, holding out his arm to me.

I take it and let him lead me back to the cabin.

After feeding me microwavable macaroni, he looks up at me. "You can take the bed—I'll sleep on the couch."

I blink, surprised by what he said.

"What? You want me to fuck you? I'd be happy to do that if you prefer."

"No," I say.

"That's what I thought."

"I wasn't afraid of you touching me. I'm just surprised you'll let me sleep alone."

"Oh, you mean that pathetic attempt at escaping?"

I frown.

"I'm not worried about you leaving," he says.

He doesn't expand, but clearly escaping isn't an option.

I shiver, the cold of the cabin getting to me. Andrea turned on a lamp, but it doesn't provide any heat. My only chance of staying warm is by getting under the covers. I'm not sure how much sleep I'll be able to get, but I need to try.

I climb into the bed, completely clothed, and watch Andrea take a blanket and pillow to the couch. He flicks off the lamp, and then I see his shadow move to the couch.

"Can I ask you a question?" he suddenly asks.

"Yes, but it doesn't mean I'll answer it."

I can sense his smile across the room. "Who would you choose? If we didn't have to play your father's games, which man would you choose? Kit, Lennox, or me?"

That's the last question I'm answering.

He chuckles through the darkness. "I see."

"You see what?"

"You give a lot away in avoiding my question."

A few minutes later, his snores echo through the room. I don't know how I fall asleep, but eventually, I do—at least until I awaken with Lennox's crooked grin smiling down at me.

CHAPTER 25

Lennox

RIALTA'S EYES cut to the couch where Andrea was sleeping.

"He's gone—outside searching for the source that set off his alarms," I say.

"And who did?"

I grin. "Hayes, Gage, and Kit."

"Kit?"

I just shrug. I'm not here to talk about Kit—at least, not unless she's finally willing to share the truth with me.

"What are you doing here?" she breathes as I straddle her. Although I'm not touching her, my breath hovers over her lips.

"I wanted to check on you—make sure Andrea isn't hurting you."

"He won't hurt me," she says.

"He did before."

She chews on her bottom lip but doesn't respond.

So he did hurt her. I squeeze my fists into tight balls to keep myself from going after Andrea. I'll murder him for touching her, for hurting her. But I'm still not sure, despite everything, how she could still choose him.

But then again, if men who hurt her were ruled out, there wouldn't be anyone left in the world for her. We have all hurt her in our own ways.

She stares at me as if she wants to say so much more but can't. I feel much the same, and I'm not going to waste this moment. I don't know how long they are going to be able to distract Andrea.

"And I want to know who you want to win."

Her eyes widen, like she's surprised by the question.

"You and everyone else."

"Did Andrea ask as well?"

"Yes."

"What did you tell him?"

"Nothing."

She raises her head, and her lips inch closer to mine, but they still don't touch.

"And what are you going to tell me?"

"Nothing—because you already know my answer."

Then our lips crash together. I don't know what's come over us. *Did she kiss me at the same time I kissed her? Or was I the one who initiated?* Either way, she's kissing me back like it's the last time—and it probably is.

My body grinds against hers. My hardness pushes against her soft curves, begging for so much more than we have time for. I know she likes sex and doesn't have a problem fucking men she's not in love with.

There are too many clothes between us—jeans and t-shirts and sweaters, but it's too cold in this cabin to get her naked and too risky if Andrea comes back. So I'll have to make do with feeling beneath her clothes. That is if she doesn't stop me earlier.

"What do you want?" I breathe as I thrust my hips between her legs, pulling a soft moan from her.

She shakes her head. "You're not going to fuck the truth out of me."

"But I am going to fuck you?"

"You better."

"Good, I need one last fuck to hold onto for eternity before I die."

She stills at my words to the point I don't feel her breathing underneath me.

I sweep my mouth over hers, kissing her and breathing into her at the same time until it sparks her to breathe again. I shouldn't have said what I said, but it was the truth, and she needed to hear it.

Her hands slip under my shirt and dig into the muscles of my back.

I deepen the kiss to keep from letting out a hiss as her fingers dig into the spots where my wounds have just started to settle in.

"Fuck, I'm sorry—" she says, pulling away from me and pulling her hands back to her sides.

I grab one of them and place it where it was on my back. "Don't be sorry. You can't cause me pain—not when we're together. Have me how you want."

She hesitantly keeps her hand on my back, gentler this time, but I don't force the issue again.

I trail my hand down her side to the hem of her shirt and push it up, feeling the softness of her belly.

Our eyes meet, and for a second, we are both thinking about the baby she carries inside. I don't know how I feel. Although I wish the baby were mine, I know it isn't. I'm terrified Rialta will suffer the same fate as Ri. I'm more afraid she'll birth the baby, only to have to hide it away like her father did her. I'm petrified she'll always be running—until death eventually catches her as it will with me.

"Don't—stop thinking, just fuck me," she says.

My eyes intensify at her words. "Such a dirty mouth."

"You taught me how."

Then I pop the button on her jeans and slip the zipper down before pushing my hand between her panties. She gasps as I find her clit with my fingers, pressing hard against the sensitive spot.

I don't have to let my fingers slip further to know how wet she is.

"I need you inside me." Her hands claw at the waistband of my jeans, trying to yank them down without undoing the button or zipper first.

She's frantic, and so am I. There's a thrill in the air at the thought of Andrea coming back in at any moment and catching us.

I lift her sweater up and lower my mouth to her nipple, swirling my tongue over her pointed tip to distract her as I undo my pants. She arches her back, her body already convulsing, and I'm not even inside her yet.

"Hurry," her voice is throaty.

Fuck me.

How am I ever supposed to give her up? How did I fail so miserably? I had her and lost her. And yet, she still wants one last time.

My cock springs free and slips between her legs, exactly where it belongs.

"Lennox," she cries as I grind my body over her slick entrance, teasing her without entering her. She's drenched, just like I knew she would be. And there's a charge of electricity in the air that heats us despite the cold.

"Get the fuck inside me, now."

I chuckle as my lips come down on hers, and she nearly strangles me as I flick her clit but still don't enter her.

"If Andrea comes back before you fuck me, I'll never forgive you. It will be the worst sin you've committed against me."

My eyes darken, and my smile drops to a serious line. "I would never let that happen."

And then I thrust inside her in a long, wicked stroke that drives her hard into the thin mattress.

Her mouth widens around my lips, but the scream she so dearly needs to leave her body is muffled by my mouth.

How could this not be enough for her to pick me? It's everything to me.

She feels so tight around me, like I fill every bit of her with my cock. Slowly, the fullness must ease enough for her to rock against me.

I rock back in slow, gentle caresses. Right now, it's not about a quick orgasm—it's about milking this moment for as long as it will last. Her body tightens around me, sucking me in before whimpering at the loss of me each time I pull almost all the way out.

"I know I'm not the greatest love of your life. I'm not even sure I'm anything to you beyond a good fuck. But you're the greatest love of my life, wifey. And it was an honor to marry you."

She opens her mouth to speak, but I shut her up by sliding two fingers into her mouth. She sucks me down until my fingers slide down the entrance to her throat.

"Fuck," she says.

Her eyes hood, and my speed quickens, every thrust moving faster and faster inside her.

And then I hear it—a whistle. The five-minute warning from Gage that Andrea is headed back.

I need to end this. I don't have time to fuck her the way I want. To clean her up afterward, to snuggle—nothing.

I grind my hips into her as I lift her legs, going deeper.

She presses her lips hard against mine as our bodies meld together with each thrust. I feel my balls tightening and the familiar feeling of my impending orgasm coming, but I'm not sure if she's close.

She nibbles on my bottom lip before biting down hard as her body writhes and explodes—gripping me like a vice grip around my cock. My own cum shoots into her as I come hard and fast. My body drains of everything I have left.

I force myself to slip out the second my orgasm stops. If I don't, I'll never leave her. And I don't have a choice but to give her up if that's what I want.

I look her in the eye, expecting a glare, a smirk, something that tells me she knows she controls my fate, and I'm about to get exactly what's coming to me. Instead, I see a bead of water roll down her cheek.

My eyes widen in fear at the sight, although I'm not sure if I'm imagining it in the darkness. I stumble back off her and scramble to pull my jeans back up.

"Are you okay?" she asks.

"Yes."

I either imagined it, or it was just sweat that fell from her brow. But it's a moment I'm going to obsess over until my last breath.

The sound of footsteps nears—I don't have much time left. So I leave her one of the last gifts I can give her.

"Take this. I'm guessing you know how to use it." I hand her a small knife—one that can easily be concealed.

She takes it from me, flicking it around in her hand like an expert who's been flinging knives at men's throats all her life. *How much did I get wrong about her? How much do I still not know?*

She pulls up her jeans before tucking the knife away in one of the pockets. I hold her gaze for a second longer, and then I disappear into the darkness.

Stepping outside, I come face to face with Andrea. He doesn't seem shocked at all to see me. I reach for my gun—preparing for a fight.

But instead, he asks, "Did you figure out who she'd choose?"

"Yes. Did you?"

"Yes."

Neither of us speaks, but the fact that Andrea isn't shooting me dead right now tells me enough. He's not as bad as I first thought. *Is he the villain I always thought he was? Or is he still tricking me into thinking he's changed while still plotting against me?*

I placed a small camera inside when I first entered, so Gage can keep an eye on Rialta and step in if Andrea tries anything.

"Keep her safe," I say as I walk into the night.

"I always do."

CHAPTER 26

Rialta

I WAKE to the smell of coffee wafting through the small cabin. Oftentimes, I wake up scared and have forgotten where I am—not this morning. I remember everything from last night. I remember Lennox.

I can still feel his lips pressed against mine. His hands gripping my body. His body pressed against mine as he thrusted inside me. I can still smell him on me, even though the overwhelming coffee smell tries to cover it up.

I sit up and find Andrea walking toward me with a coffee, banana, and jar of peanut butter. He tosses the banana and peanut butter on the bed next to me and then hands me the cup of coffee.

I raise an eyebrow. "Can't cook?"

"I can cook; there are just very limited supplies here."

I sip my coffee as he goes back to grab his own cup. I begin on the banana, dipping it into the peanut butter. I'm going to need my strength today.

Andrea sits on the armrest of the couch as he stares at me.

"What now?" I ask.

He shrugs. "I don't know."

I frown. "So your plan is just to keep me here indefinitely?"

"I guess."

I narrow my eyes and take another sip of my coffee before I speak. "You didn't have sex with me."

His brows jump. "What?"

"You didn't fuck me."

"So? I didn't know that you wanted me that badly after everything that happened. But I'd be happy to oblige if that's what you want."

"You didn't fuck me last night. You haven't tried this morning. And that time we were together—you didn't fuck me then, either. You drugged me to confuse me. You made it look like we were fucking to Lennox and drugged him so that he'd think you did too. But you didn't, not really."

He stills.

I'm right.

"You haven't tried to cause me to miscarry."

"Maybe because I don't believe you're actually pregnant. I see no signs of a baby."

"No, that's not it."

He crosses his arms and smirks down at me. "Then what is it? Since you can read my mind and all. Tell me what I'm thinking. What's my plan?"

"I don't know. I just know you're not the monster you pretend to be."

"I'm not?" He cocks his head to the side and looks down at me with amusement dancing in his eyes.

"No, you're not. You say you want to kill Lennox. And yet, you didn't when you had the chance."

"And when did I have the chance?"

"Don't—I know you know that Lennox was here last night. You had to have run into each other outside. I heard you two talking, and it smells like sex in here. You know. And you didn't kill him. Why?"

He glares down at me, trying to shut me up with just a look. But I'm not afraid of him.

And then he pounces. He's on top of me in a second. My coffee is knocked out of my hand, and my arms are pinned above my head as his other hand goes to my throat. My legs are spread, and he smashes his core between my legs.

"And what do you think now?" he growls.

"It's all an act. You still aren't going to fuck me."

He laughs maniacally.

"I'll do much worse."

I wiggle one hand free and grab the knife Lennox left me. Pressing it against his throat, I whisper in his ear.

"No, you won't."

Andrea won't hurt me, but he also won't tell me the truth. I'm close to piecing it all together, but time is running out.

CHAPTER 27

Lennox

"YOU HAVE TO BE PATIENT. These things take time," I say for the millionth time as Kit paces our hotel room.

"I don't understand why your men haven't figured out who The Abyss is yet. It can't be that difficult to find a man who has been hunting this family for years."

I roll my eyes. "If it was easy, you would have already found him."

"I would if you would ever let me leave this damn hotel room."

I chuckle from the chair I'm sitting in while I drink a beer. It's been a week since I last saw Rialta, and I'm getting antsy too, but I don't tell Kit that. "You leave this hotel room, you're dead. Between The Abyss, Andrea, and Vincent's men—one of them will take you out before you get ten feet from the building."

Kit shakes his head. "Then let me go. I'd be one less competitor for you to worry about."

"Yes, but then Rialta would never forgive me for letting you die. So it's a lose-lose for me."

Kit huffs, and then there's a knock on the door.

We both whip our heads to it. I pull out my gun. Kit just stands frozen. He really does have a death wish.

"Gun," I hiss at him. He fumbles for the gun in his waistband.

I walk to the door, keeping my gun pointed at it. I look through the peephole and find no one there.

My brow furrows as I ease the door open. Whoever knocked is gone, but there's a white envelope lying on the ground.

I pick it up and then quickly shut and re-lock the door. The hotel has a standard mid-budget lock on it that won't hold up if anyone wants to get inside. But that's not why I chose this hotel room anyway.

"What is it?" Kit asks.

I pull out a picture from the envelope, and my heart sinks.

"What?" Kit asks again, his voice higher this time.

I hold out the photo, and he gasps at the sight.

"Is she marrying him? Did he win?"

As I stare at the photo of Rialta in a wedding dress, memories of her walking down the aisle to marry me flash through my head. All the blood drains from my body as reality sinks in.

"Are you okay, man?"

"Fine," I snap.

He chuckles. "She doesn't love him. He can't win. Vincent gave her a choice."

"Vincent gave her the appearance of a choice. She won't have a choice when he's the only one left standing, and we're both dead."

Kit's face pales. "What do we do?"

I flip the photo over to find an address written. It's a

trap; I know it is. He wouldn't have sent us this photo otherwise. And I recognize the address as the same church Rialta and I got married in—the bastard.

"We go to the address."

———

I open the doors, and it's like stepping through my memories. I'm calmer this time than last. Before was a beginning—this is an ending.

Kit stands to my right. His body shaking in a subtle rage or fear. I can't tell with him.

I contacted Gage and Hayes, but it seems their phone has been turned off. I have no way to contact them anymore. It was to be expected when they went back to the Retribution Kings. I just have to hope they were accepted into the fold and not killed.

But it means I'm on my own, and this church may be the last place I see before I die.

I know why Andrea called us here—to end this. I don't know if he's succeeded in figuring out who The Abyss is yet. Or if he's persuaded Rialta to pick him over the two of us. But he must think he has the pieces to end this tonight.

When I look up, all I see is her in a cascade of white fabric. The dress is big—so big I don't know how she can move in the skirts of fabric. But maybe that's the point— keep her immobilized as the prize to be won.

It makes me sick.

Rialta Corsi deserves so much better. Even if the man she wants wins, she doesn't deserve to be forced into anything. She doesn't deserve all her choices to be taken. Her father may have committed crimes that he needs to face punishment for, but not her.

Her eyes travel down the aisle to Kit, then me. Kit probably sees his future wife when he looks at her, but I see a warrior who is finally going to take her future into her own hands.

Kit begins walking down the center aisle without a care in the world, while I cautiously stalk, trying to sniff out the danger.

"You look beautiful," Kit says, and I find myself rolling my eyes once again. It seems that's all I do in response to him.

Rialta helplessly looks over at me as Kit tries to figure out how to get close enough to hug her without stepping on her dress. Her look splits my soul in half, and I stumble back, unsure of what I'm going to do next. He hugs her over her dress half-heartedly.

"You came," Andrea says from behind Rialta.

"Of course, we fucking came. We weren't going to let you force Rialta into marrying you," Kit spits in his direction while still gripping onto Rialta.

"I'm not going to force Rialta into marrying anyone. She agreed to marry whoever wins," Andrea says.

"What is he talking about?" Kit asks Rialta.

Rialta looks at him with a serious expression. "If you're to be my husband, then you have to beat them. You have to be the strongest man. You have to be able to protect me and my unborn baby. You have to be able to do the job too."

Kit blinks as if he can't believe what he's hearing. In the blink of a second, he went from having my help and being a frontrunner to having a one-in-three chance.

"I'm confused. Are you saying you want to decide who marries Rialta with a challenge different than what Vincent proposed?" I ask, looking at Andrea.

"None of us are going to be able to find and kill The Abyss in the amount of time Vincent is giving us. What

Vincent really cares about is that we are loyal to Rialta and will continue the Corsi bloodline," he clarifies.

I nod, agreeing. Vincent just wants someone who will keep Rialta safe, and falling in love with her would ensure that.

"What are you proposing?" I ask.

"A fight without weapons," Rialta says.

"To the death?" Kit asks.

"To whenever you surrender or die, yes. But if you surrender, the others agree to let you go. You get to live. And we'll make Vincent think you've been killed to satisfy his terms. You'd be free if you surrender," Rialta says.

There it is—a way for her to save us all. She cares about us all in different ways and doesn't want to see any of us die. But she only loves one of us.

Andrea walks to the first pew and begins unloading his guns and knives onto the seat.

I walk next to him and begin doing the same.

When we've both finished, we look to Kit. He's the only one who hasn't agreed to this. It wouldn't be in his interest to agree to this challenge. But he can't win Vincent's challenge either because he'll never be able to find and kill The Abyss. None of us can complete Vincent's challenge for different reasons, so this is the only way to settle it. If Kit wants to surrender, he can. And if Rialta tells me she chooses Kit, I'll make sure he wins.

Kit leans into Rialta, his lips sweeping against hers. From where I'm standing, I can't tell if she kisses him back or not. When the kiss ends, he walks over to us and tosses his gun into the pile.

"That's it?" Andrea asks.

"That's it." Kit glares at me. "That's all this asshole would give me."

Andrea chuckles, and I smirk. Glancing over at Rialta, I swear I see a hint of a smile creeping up her face too.

"Rules?" Kit asks.

"No weapons. Everything else is fair game. When one of us surrenders, we let them go as long as they promise to disappear forever," Andrea says.

"And if no one surrenders?" Kit asks.

I have the same thought. But whether this works or not, there's enough pent-up frustration between the three of us that it would be helpful to beat the shit out of each other.

No one answers. We'll have to decide that if we come to it.

"Then let the best man win," Rialta says with distaste in her mouth, clearly hating being a prize to be won.

I expected Kit to be the first one to throw a punch. What I didn't expect was for him to land a blow to my jaw that has me tasting blood.

Andrea throws a punch to my stomach that takes my breath away before I can react to Kit. I'm a pretty good fighter, but after everything I've been through these past few days, I'm not as quick at anticipating punches as I used to be.

I block another punch from Andrea, while Kit gets a kick into my ribs. Blow and after blow hits me.

I don't know why the two of them are ganging up on me, but I need to do something to change the direction of this, or I'll be out in a matter of minutes. And if I'm going to die, it's going to be because Rialta wants me dead.

I sweep Kit's feet out from underneath him and then tackle Andrea to the ground. Finally, I get a good punch in before closing my hands around his throat, strangling him.

He grips my wrists, trying to remove my hands, but I squeeze harder. I don't know when I'll get an advantage like this again, so I use everything in me to get him to surrender.

There was a time when I wanted to kill him, but now I think I'd prefer he'd just surrender.

Andrea's eyes bulge after his head whips toward Rialta's direction.

Kit has his arm wrapped around her waist and a gun in his hand.

I release Andrea immediately and ease off him. Of course, Kit didn't fight fair—he kept a gun on him. The cheater.

Andrea and I both stand up carefully, trying to decide how we take him down. Maybe we should both surrender now before he kills us. He doesn't care about the rules. He doesn't care to fight honorably.

I guess if that was the only chance he had to win the woman he loves, then I'd understand. But thinking about how well he fought, he had a real chance of winning.

Kit stands smugly behind Rialta with his fingers splayed across her lower belly like he's already won.

He points the gun at Andrea. "Do you surrender?"

Andrea doesn't look at him. He looks to Rialta as if he's waiting for her to tell him what to do.

I furrow my brow in confusion.

"Yes," Andrea finally breathes.

"Good, then I'll spare you if you find and kill The Abyss by the end of the week."

"That's impossible," Andrea says.

"Find someone, anyone who can fit the description and frame them then. I don't care. But we need Vincent to think he's dead."

I frown. That plan won't work, but Andrea nods and cautiously walks out of the church a free man.

I'm up next.

"Kneel," Kit says to me.

I do.

"I'm not going to ask you to surrender. I'm not going to ask if you want a chance to live—I already know how Rialta feels about you. She hates you and blames you for her situation. You'd kill me and our child the first chance you get."

I don't respond.

I know how this is going to end, and I've accepted it.

I started this mission for love, and so it shall end with love.

I never thought I'd fall in love with Rialta Corsi. I never thought I could love again after Iris. If I'd asked the younger version of myself if I could survive two great loves in my life, I'd answer no. But loving Rialta, even if she never expressed that love back, has been worth everything. And dying to make sure she gets to live happily married is the only way I can imagine leaving this earth.

"Let me. I want to be the one to kill Lennox," Rialta says with a vicious glare at me.

"No, I have to be the one to kill him. It's the only way Vincent will take me seriously," Kit says.

I keep my gaze on Rialta, ignoring Kit. I'll either die while looking at her or...

Rialta's hand dives into the front of her dress, pulling something out at the same time Kit pulls the trigger.

It all happened so fast that I'm not sure what happened. *Was I shot?* I don't feel anything, but sometimes it takes a minute for the pain to register.

After quickly examining my body and finding nothing, I finally look at Kit. His face is ghost-white, and his eyes are bulging wide as he groans.

Rialta pushes him to his knees, and blood rushes down his throat from the knife she's thrust into it.

Kit and I are both kneeling, both in awe of her for very different reasons.

Rialta yanks the knife out of his throat, and I wince. She

grips the knife in her hand as she walks to his front, staring him down as his blood drips onto her wedding dress.

She grabs his chin and tilts it up, forcing him to look her in the eyes.

"I thought you were my friend. My first crush. The love of my life. I would have done anything for you. I would have run away with you and given up the family that just came back into my life." She shakes her head, and tears stream down her face.

"But I was a fool. You were never any of those things. You were a plant—your gang, the Crimson Cartel, placed you in my life the second they found me. Instead of killing me, like you did the rest of my family, you decided the better route was to make me fall in love with you. Marrying me and becoming Vincent's heir would give you the best opportunity to destroy us from within."

Kit glares at her as he opens his mouth to speak, but blood pours out his mouth instead.

She flashes a wicked smirk. "You don't get to speak, not anymore. You're The Abyss. Your father was first, but when he died, you took over. And you've taken enough from my family."

She grabs his hair with one hand and slices the knife across his neck. Blood sprays onto her dress before he collapses. A second later, he's gone.

I'm still kneeling as I stare up at Rialta Corsi—a woman who has lived up to the family name. She has become a Corsi in every way that matters. I've never seen her stronger or more beautiful than right now.

My eyes are filled with awe as she turns and faces me.

I could face the same fate as him. She could stab that knife into my chest as easily as she did him. She could kill us all and force her father to realize she doesn't need a man by her side—that she alone can be his heir.

She has a choice. My heart thumps wildly in my chest because I know which choice I want her to make. Stepping toward me, Rialta's tongue sweeps across her lips like as if about to devour me.

"Lennox, I love you too."

CHAPTER 28

Rialta

AS LENNOX KNEELS in front of me, I can't tell if he's in shock from seeing me slit a man's throat or shock from me finally telling him I love him.

"Stand up," I command.

He does automatically, and I'm still not sure he realizes the truth—I love him, and I've always loved him. I don't know even where to start in telling him everything, so I say the only thing that comes to mind.

"Thank you for the knife. It was useful."

He chuckles. "You are something else."

"Something good?" I inch toward him.

He steps toward me. "Something amazing."

I blush.

Then his hands are on my hips, our breathing sinked, and our eyes locked. We each moisten our lips at the same time.

"Kiss me," I say.

He growls. "I've waited so long to hear you say that."

"Kiss me," I say again, and he does. He yanks me to him,

the fabric of the dress bunching up between us as his lips devour me in a deep, loving kiss.

He pulls away enough to say. "Not the kiss you part, the other part."

"Oh," I blush again.

His eyes blaze down at me until I say it again.

"I love you, Lennox. I've loved you as long as you've loved me. I'm sorry I didn't say it sooner."

Before I can say more, his lips are on me again. The kiss takes my breath away, and it's something I wasn't sure I was going to get to experience again.

"Can I borrow this?" Lennox asks, pointing to the knife I'm still gripping like my life depends on it.

I nod.

He takes the knife and plunges it into the dress at my waist.

I gasp but grin as I watch him cut away yards of fabric from this dress.

"Whose idea was it to wear this thing?" Lennox asks as he pulls away more and more fabric.

"Andrea's."

Lennox shakes his head. "I'll deal with him later for this."

I smirk.

After freeing my legs from the dress, Lennox lifts me by my thighs, and I wrap my arms and legs around him. He steps over the remains of my dress and then over Kit's dead body, carrying me up to the altar.

Our tongues tangle together in kiss after kiss. He slams my back against the cool of a stained glass window.

"I've missed you, wifey." And I know he means more than just my body. He misses the open truth between us, as have I.

He arches my neck to one side so he can kiss down my

throat. Goosebumps rush through my body as his mouth dips lower. He kisses the sensitive spot over my clavicle and then lower still to the curve of my breast.

"I never thought I'd get to do this again."

"You'll get this forever. But only if you stop teasing me and get your thick cock inside me."

"My greedy wife," he chuckles.

I love that he continues to call me his wife. Despite all the evidence I gave him, he never gave up on us, and I love that. He refused to believe I didn't love him, and he carried our love all this time as much as I did.

"I'm sorry, I shouldn't call you wife until after we've talked," he says suddenly.

"No."

His heart sinks, and he stops kissing me.

"I mean, no, don't stop calling me that."

He gives me a half smile, but I smash my lips against his to reassure him. If he'd get inside me, he'd realize we are one, and there is no way to separate us.

I paw at his waistband, practically ripping his jeans in half with my bare hands to get to him. At the same time, he pushes the remainder of my dress aside to find my clit. He rubs over the sensitive flesh until I'm dripping down my inner thigh.

"Husband," I croon.

He bucks his body against me as I call him that, his cock slipping between my thighs.

I don't let him drag this out. I'm so needy, so desperate to feel him connected to me in the deepest way. I grab his cock and press him against my entrance just before he thrusts hard into me all at once.

We both shudder, finally feeling what we've needed all this time. It's not like last time. This isn't a goodbye. This is a union of our bodies forever.

He begins thrusting in and out, slamming my body into the glass wall over and over.

"I'm sorry I didn't tell you sooner. It killed me not to tell you I loved you every time I saw you. But I was trying to keep you alive," I say.

"I know."

"I'm sorry."

"Don't be, but you could have told me in secret."

"I needed you to believe I hated you so you would stay away and alive, you fool."

He pulls my bottom lip into his mouth, and my entire body is filled with him.

"I never loved Kit after we were married, after I fell in love with you. I never strayed. It was always you."

"I know, wifey, I know."

Then he fucks me like he knows. No words are needed. He fucks me so hard to tell me everything inside him—he belongs to me, he'd do anything for me, he'd kill any man. Lennox would go to hell and back for me.

I've never been fucked so forcefully in my life. Each drive of his cock inside me fills me with everything I've been denying myself, and when he pulls almost all the way out, I'm shattered by the temporary emptiness.

Lennox's eyes sear into mine as his lips hungrily devour me. Neither of us could've held in this feeling much longer. We have too much pent-up longing to keep it inside.

"Come all over me, wifey. Come and let go of all of the pain."

I can barely speak, let alone do anything but come all over his cock. Still, I force myself to get the words out. I vow to say the words as many times as I can until I'm sure he believes them.

"Fuck, I love you, Lennox."

My words have him coming deep inside me. His warm cum fills me until I can feel it dripping down my inner thigh.

I feel myself sliding down the wall, and he tightens his grip on my ass, holding me up.

We're both grinning like fools in love as he rests his head against my forehead. Finally, I feel like we can tackle anything together.

Lennox slowly pulls out before easing me down to my feet. We're a mess covered in blood, sweat, and cum. My dress is ripped. His jeans are still down. But we have eyes for nothing but each other.

"We don't have much time before Vincent and Andrea and anyone else gets here, and we'll have to face reality, but I want you to know something first," he says.

I nod, holding my breath in doubt.

He smiles, shaking his head. "Stop those thoughts at once." He kisses me tenderly, and I melt into him.

"All I'm going to say is you're the strongest person I know. And no matter what Vincent or anyone else says, you always have a choice, and that includes whether you stay married to me or any man. You always have a choice."

CHAPTER 29

Lennox

THIS IS A DREAM; it has to be. I still can't believe Rialta Corsi loves me. But she does.

I've known the truth for a while, but it was never my decision to make. I had to trust Rialta to know how to handle this dangerous situation, and she did. She saved us all.

There are so many details to be explained, and the danger isn't over until Vincent agrees, but I have hope again at last.

The church doors fly open, and Rialta and I jump closer into each other's arms as our heads whip in that direction.

Vincent walks in, followed by Andrea. Neither of them gives away anything going on in their heads.

Vincent stops in front of Kit's body and looks up to us, his expression blank. Then he says, "Well done, Andrea."

"Thank you, sir," Andrea responds.

I furrow my brow in confusion. "Thank you, Andrea? Really? Andrea did nothing. Rialta was the one who figured out Kit has been hunting your family and killed him. Not Andrea!"

Andrea's lips turn up in a smile as he stares at Rialta. Rialta gives him a small nod back, and I swear her lips are turning into a hint of a smile. *I'm definitely missing something.*

I want to pull her tighter to my side, but if I've learned anything, it's that she's not mine to control. She has to make her own decisions, so I won't force anything.

"I tasked Andrea with testing your relationship," Vincent says.

"What?" Rialta and I say at the same time.

"I could see Lennox was the perfect man for you, Rialta, but I knew that you wouldn't accept him simply because I chose him." He turns to me. "I could also see that Lennox was resistant to falling in love. I didn't know why, and I don't care to now, but I knew in order for your relationship to have a chance at working, you needed some prodding."

"You already gave me tasks to ensure our relationship worked. You didn't need to add Andrea to the mix," I grit out between my teeth.

"I did. You were going to fail—"

"The Abyss is dead. I wouldn't have failed."

"Yes, the Abyss is dead. But you didn't think you were capable of falling in love. I could see you trying to find a way to back out. Both of you were fighting your love for one another. And I would do anything to protect my daughter, so the push was an easy decision."

I open my mouth to speak, but Rialta puts her hand on my chest, stopping me.

"I didn't need a push—I needed the ability to make my own choices. I'll never forgive you for what you did," she says.

"I don't need your forgiveness. I need you safe and alive." Vincent looks from her to me and then back to her. "And you're safe now."

"I was always safe. I'm the one who killed the Abyss, not Lennox. *Me*. I protected myself. I schemed and figured out how to keep the man I love safe because I was terrified of you or Andrea killing him. I sacrificed everything, and none of it was necessary. You could have protected me, kept me from having to kill a man, and you didn't."

Vincent's eyes widen at the sight of Kit and the realization that his daughter was the one to slaughter him.

"How did you piece it together?" Andrea asks.

"Kit was too skilled for the boy I grew up with. He shouldn't have known how to fight or use a gun, but he did. He tried to hide it, but it was too obvious." Rialta's eyes water. "He pretended to be kidnapped and faked his injuries. He took River. He tortured her, trying to figure out if I was pregnant or not. It was no longer enough for him to simply kill everyone; he wanted to keep one heir alive to continue the torture. And when she wouldn't tell him—he caused her to miscarry."

Tears drip down her cheeks, but she's never looked stronger as she continues. "Kit said he loved me, but he didn't. I didn't realize it until I fell in love with Lennox and knew there was nothing I wouldn't do for him, including giving him up to keep him alive. So that's what I did. I tried to force Lennox to leave so you wouldn't kill him. I hate you and wish you were dead just like Kit for making me terrified for Lennox's life."

I tuck my arm over her shoulder and give her a squeeze. She leans into my chest.

"You're both going to be constantly afraid for each other for the rest of your lives. Even if you get out, even if you run for it like your sister is, this world will catch up with you one day. And you both need to know that you're strong enough to face whatever happens. Now you know that. You know you're strong enough together. You're strong enough to have babies and to make the tough choices when it comes to my empire. You can hate me for it, but I'll sleep soundly with my decision," Vincent explains.

We both glare at Vincent. He's a cruel man. He doesn't get his reputation for nothing.

Rialta wants to kill him. He's put her through hell but now isn't the time. We just got our life back—I'm not going to ruin it by letting either of us kill Vincent.

"You took things too far," I glare at Andrea.

Now it's Rialta's turn to hold me back. "He didn't."

"He fucked you. He hurt you. He—"

"He didn't do any of those things. He did hurt you, and I'm so sorry for it. But he didn't touch me."

"I saw him. I saw—"

"You were drugged. It was easy to make you believe whatever we wanted you to believe. He didn't fuck me. He drugged me too, and just pretended to have sex with me. I guess we both wanted to pushed you to the brink. Me to get you to hate me, to divorce me, to run away and be safe. And Andrea pushed you to follow Vincent's orders—thinking you'd fall even more in love with me and stay with me forever."

I narrow my eyes in Andrea's direction.

"I understand if you want to kill me or fire me at the very least, when you take over the Corsi empire, but I'd be happy to serve you as your right-hand man, Lennox. You are truly worthy of the job," Andrea says.

And for some reason, I immediately trust Andrea as much as I trust Hayes or Gage or Beckett. But I'll leave that for another time.

Vincent looks to me. "I accept you as my heir, as my daughter's husband. You have fulfilled your end of our deal. When I die, everything I have is yours."

And then Vincent walks out of the church as Rialta and I cling to one another.

"Should I clean up this mess, or are you going to kill me?" Andrea asks me.

I look to Rialta. "It's your choice who lives and dies. It's always been your choice."

She looks to Andrea. "Clean up the mess. Clean up all of our messes, and we might let you live."

Andrea nods with a small smirk on his lips as he begins cleaning up.

"Andrea taught you how to fight?" I ask her.

"Yes, I didn't know before. But I asked him, and he taught me. I wasn't hiding some persona from you. I truly didn't know how to do anything before Hayes gave me that first lesson, and then you taught me how to be brave. Andrea just taught me the mechanics."

"I'm grateful."

She nods, looking at Andrea.

And then she looks back at me. "Take me home, husband."

CHAPTER 30

Rialta

I'M SITTING on the edge of Lennox's bed with a box of pregnancy tests I keep flipping over in my hands. It's been three days since we came back to Lennox's apartment, and we've barely left the bed, barely faced reality.

Lennox ran out to get us some food, and I found this box in the bathroom. It seems I wasn't the only one thinking we needed these.

The apartment feels just the same as before I left. It's my safe place. It feels like Lennox. But it's also different because everyone else is gone.

Hayes and Gage are back with the Retribution Kings. There's a lot more to their story, but Lennox hasn't shared much yet. He's only told me they're with the Retribution Kings, so now we're enemies. Hopefully, when we take over the Corsi men, we can reach an alliance with the Retribution Kings.

It's hard not to see them, but I'm hoping we can make things right soon enough. Missing them isn't going to be as hard as missing River and Beckett. She left me a note saying she didn't know how long they'd be gone, just that they needed to get away. They needed time to figure out what they wanted and to heal from the trauma they experienced.

I know they still want a child, but I'm not sure how they'd manage coming back and having a baby, not after what they went through. They both deserve to be happy more than anyone I know. The only way they'll be happy is by having a baby, so I don't expect to ever see them again.

I turn the box over again, and then I feel him. I don't have to look up to know Lennox is standing at the top of the stairs watching me.

He doesn't say anything as he walks over and sits on the edge of the bed next to me. I can smell the bag of food he puts down next to his feet, but food is the last thing I want right now.

He waits patiently at my side for me to speak.

"Who's the girl whose name is tattooed on your heart?"

He blinks, not expecting me to ask that question. He probably thinks the name is concealed. To most people it would be, but not to me when I've had a chance to examine every inch of his body.

He exhales slowly. "Her name is Lila." He looks at me with pain in his eyes. "I lied when I told you my story earlier. Or at least, I changed a few details. And I'm sorry—it was too painful to share. It's still too painful." He pauses and then forces the words out. "Lila was my daughter."

I gasp. Of all the things I thought he might say, I wasn't expecting that.

Tears fall freely from his eyes as memories roll through him. I wish I didn't have to drag up so much pain to understand him more.

I grip his hand.

He takes a deep, shuttering breath, and then he continues. "It was during initiation. Iris and I were being initiated. Our daughter was ten months old. She was just starting to walk, and she had a laugh that made my heart sing every time I heard it. She was a beautiful little girl. She had my eyes and her mother's dark hair."

"It's okay, you don't have to tell me." I feel ashamed for asking him. I knew he was hiding something, and I didn't want there to be any more secrets between us, but I never thought it would be something this painful. I can't even imagine what he's been through. I'm not sure how he shoulders it.

"I do. I want you to know." Lennox looks me in the eyes. "We left Lila with Iris's cousin for the week. And when we came back, Lila was gone."

I can't stay strong for Lennox. I can't hold back my own tears. I sob, pulling Lennox into a hug. We both sob and sob and sob over the loss of his daughter until finally, I gather the strength to ask more questions.

"Who? How?"

"Her cousin took her swimming. She drowned. It was a fluke accident. I failed her. I should have been there to protect her. Instead, I was pretending I was strong at the initiation. That I was worthy of being a Retribution King when I should have been focused on being a father."

"You didn't fail her," I say, touching his cheek.

He grips my hand, stopping me from comforting him. "Except, I did. I should have never agreed to the initiation. I shouldn't have left her with anyone at such a young age."

"It's not your fault. It was a fluke accident. It could have happened to anyone. But it's terrible all the same."

"It's my fault. I'll never forgive myself."

"And Iris?"

"She died of a broken heart, not during initiation like I said. Her immune system was weak, and she got sickness after sickness after losing Lila—until finally, her body couldn't survive any longer. Her heart just gave out."

"I'm so sorry, Lennox. If I could take away your pain, I would. No one should have to endure that." I stare down at the box in my hand, even more racked with nerves than I was before.

He stares at the box too.

"You never confirmed you were pregnant?"

"No. My period is just late, and I've had lots of symptoms, but in the last three days, I'm more unsure than ever. I just told you I was pregnant with Kit's child to get you to hurt you. To get you to leave. To keep you safe."

He nods.

"But I'm terrified to take a test. You deserve to have a child and—"

"Stop—stop worrying. It's not my choice. It's entirely yours."

I shake my head. "No, it's ours."

He grips the sides of my head with his hands, and his thumbs wipe the tears from my cheeks. "I love you, Rialta. I'll love you whether you're pregnant or not. Whether the baby is Kit's or mine. Whether you decide to have the baby or not. I love you. I choose you. I'm not the one who has to carry the baby or birth it."

"Yes, but I want to know how you feel. I know you'd make a great father if I am pregnant."

"As you would make a great mother. But us being good parents doesn't mean that we have to have a baby."

"But Vincent—"

"No, we are not thinking about what Vincent wants. He doesn't deserve to have heirs. And if we decide not to have children, then we will deal with him later."

I nod, still unsure of how I feel. No, that's not true. I'm afraid to speak my feelings out loud now that I know Lennox's history.

Lennox sets the box down on the bed next to me and takes my hands in his. He kisses them both.

"Forget about everything. Forget about my past. Forget about Vincent or Kit. Forget about wondering whose baby it is if you are pregnant. If it was just us and we lived a normal life, would our happily ever after include a baby?"

Lennox stares at me with such emotion and love in his eyes. His look tells me no matter what I say, he's not going to stop loving me.

"No, it wouldn't include a baby. I've never wanted to be a mother."

He leans in and kisses me tenderly on the lips. "Thank you for your honesty."

"What about you? Do you want a child?"

"No, and I'm not just saying that because it's what you want to hear. It's the truth. I loved Lila with all my heart, but I never imagined myself as a father. And while I'd be happy to raise a child with you if that's what you wanted, I don't need to be a father. And no child I have would ever replace Lila."

"You're sure? Because if you need a child to be happy, I'll gladly have a child with you."

"I'm more than sure."

She kisses me, our lips melding together as our words sink in. Neither of us wants to be parents.

When we pull apart, she stares at the box of pregnancy tests again. "Take a test if you want, but it's your choice to be pregnant. If you don't want to be pregnant, it won't matter what the test says."

"I love you so fucking much."

"I love you too, wifey."

"I'll take the test later, and we can decide what we are going to do then. But right now, I just want to be with my husband."

He growls. "I like that idea. How do you want me to fuck you?"

I rake my teeth over my bottom lip. It's always my choice with him. I never realized how much I needed an equal and how much he is that equal in every way.

We have a task ahead of us in dealing with Vincent. And Lennox will be seen as the head of the Corsi line when Vincent dies, but Lennox will always see me as his equal. He'll never make a decision without me, and we won't hide anything from each other ever again.

I blush. "I think you know me well enough by now. I trust you to decide the best way to fuck me."

His eyes grow devious, and his tongue licks over me. "How about page forty-three?"

"Forty-three?" I shake my head, not having a clue what he's talking about. Then I remember he still has my journal with my dirtiest fantasies inside. But I have no idea what I wrote on page forty-three. "Whatever it is, I want you to do it."

He grins wickedly. "My pleasure, wifey."

A few minutes later, I'm naked with my arms tied to my calves with rope. A camera is pointed at me as I writhe on my knees and cheek on the bed, waiting for Lennox to reenter the bedroom. I don't know what he's planning on doing with the tape, but I'm already dripping and panting with need for him.

And I can't wait for him to fulfill every fantasy in my journal. Although, I might need to snatch it back so I can add a few new fantasies to it.

"You ready for me, wifey?" Lennox says from the top of the stairs. He's wearing nothing but his dark jeans and a devouring wolfish grin.

"Yes, I'm always ready for you."

I GLANCE at my phone to check the time. It's five past eleven, exactly when we said we would meet.

I nurse my whiskey as I sit in the back booth of the crowded bar. I'm not sure if they'll show up or if they even received my message. But I'll wait until I finish my drink at least before I give up on them. It's important that we speak.

Suddenly, two men slide into my booth. It takes me a second to even recognize them. Hayes has the hood of his sweatshirt over his hair, and he's lost his signature glasses. Unless a lot has changed, he can't see shit right now, as I know he refuses to wear contacts. And Gage is wearing a baseball cap over his buzzed head and sunglasses.

"Thanks for meeting me," I say.

"Of course, but I'll send you a new protocol from now on to arrange meetings," Gage says.

I nod. I doubt we will need to chat again for a while, but it's probably best.

"How have you two been? Is everything okay with the Retribution Kings?"

"If you're asking if we are ready for phase two of the plan, then yes," Hayes answers.

I want to get straight to the point, but I bite my tongue, keeping from speaking.

"Rialta finally tell you that she loves you?" Hayes teases.

"Yes. We're happy together. And Vincent has made me his heir."

"Good, then phase one is complete," Gage says.

I nod, feeling uneasy for not including Rialta in this meeting, from hiding things from her. But she can never know the truth; it would risk everything.

"You set up Kit?" I ask.

"Yes," Gage answers.

"So, he was innocent?"

"No, he wasn't innocent. The evidence we planted for Rialta to find was true—he belonged to the Crimson Cartel. They found out where Vincent sent Rialta and planted him in her life. Told him to make her fall for him so he could marry her and take over the Corsi men. He wasn't innocent—"

"He's just not The Abyss," I finish.

"No, he's not," Hayes confirms.

I hesitate before speaking. "Are we sure we want to continue the plan now that—"

"Yes," Hayes and Gage each say.

Hayes looks to Gage, and he explains. "Yes, we agreed at the beginning of this that no matter what, we would continue to the end. So we are continuing with or without you."

"I'm with you, of course. I'm with you," I say.

"Good," Gage says as he studies me closely.

Hayes smiles tightly.

"Just tell me what you need from me, and I'll do it," I say.

"For now, just be happy with Rialta and stay on Vincent's good side. We'll let you know when the next step is completed. Can you do that?" Hayes asks.

I grin. "Take as long as you need for phase two. I have no problem being very, very happy with Rialta. I'm thankful this plan led me to her. It was like we were meant for each other. Even if everything else fails, I'm happy for it bringing me her."

"I'm glad your feelings for each other are real, and I hope this plan doesn't ruin your relationship," Hayes says.

"It won't. Nothing will ever tear us apart." This plan used to be the most important thing to me. It was the only thing keeping me going. But now, all I care about is loving Rialta and keeping her safe. So if it comes down to choosing between the plan and Rialta—I know who I'm picking, no matter the cost.

———

Thank you for reading Lennox & Rialta's story! I hope you enjoyed it! Want to read Hayes's story and find out more about the secrets the guys share? Read Hayes & Lilith's story in HAYES

One-click HAYES Here

I'm the sunshine of our group. The funny one. The good-looking one. The one who never takes life too seriously. But now it's time for me to complete my mission. Lennox and Gage deserve it. I'll complete my mission quickly, so we can soon put our dark past behind us. And I was so close to succeeding, until I met Lilith. She's the darkness to my sunshine. The grumpiest, most irritating woman. Falling for

Lilith is going to destroy me, but I can't help falling anyway...

JOIN ELLA'S NEWSLETTER & NEVER MISS A SALE OR NEW RELEASE → ellamiles.com/freebooks

TRUTH OR LIES:

Taken by Lies #1

Betrayed by Truths #2

Trapped by Lies #3

Stolen by Truths #4

Possessed by Lies #5

Consumed by Truths #6

SINFUL TRUTHS:

Sinful Truth #1

Twisted Vow #2

Reckless Fall #3

Tangled Promise #4

Fallen Love #5

Broken Anchor #6

LIES SERIES:

Lies We Share: A Prologue #0.5

Vicious Lies #1

Desperate Lies #2

Fated Lies #3

Cruel Lies #4

Dangerous Lies #5

Endless Lies #6

RETRIBUTION GAMES SERIES:

Mistaken Hero #1

Forbidden Princess #2

Tempted Hero #3

Fatal Princess #4

Tortured Hero #5

Dangerous Princess #6

RETRIBUTION KINGS SERIES:

Lennox #1

PRETEND SERIES:

Pretend I'm Yours

Pretend We're Over

Pretend: The Complete Series

DIRTY SERIES:

Dirty Obsession

Dirty Addiction

Dirty Revenge

Dirty: The Complete Series

ALIGNED SERIES:

Aligned: Volume 1

Aligned: Volume 2

Aligned: Volume 3

Aligned: Volume 4

Aligned: The Complete Series Boxset

UNFORGIVABLE SERIES:

Heart of a Thief

Heart of a Liar

Heart of a Prick

Unforgivable: The Complete Series Boxset

MAYBE, DEFINITELY SERIES:

Maybe Yes

Maybe Never

Maybe Always

Maybe: The Complete Series

Definitely Yes

Definitely No

Definitely Forever

Definitely: The Complete Series

STANDALONES:

Finding Perfect

Savage Love

Too Much

Not Sorry

Hate Me or Love Me: An Enemies to Lovers Romance Collection